# A Possible Esoteric Tale

# A Possible Esoteric Tale
## Michael Sousa

© Michael Sousa
A Possible Esoteric Tale

"All rights reserved. Unless otherwise provided by law, the total or partial reproduction of this work, nor its incorporation into a computer system, nor its transmission in any form or by any means (electronic, mechanical, photocopying, recording or others) is not permitted without the prior written authorisation of the copyright holders. Violation of such rights entails legal sanctions and may constitute an offense against intellectual property."

*"Eritis sicut Dii, scientes Bonum et Malum"* – The Serpent

# Summary

1. Prologue: Under the Heat of Dead Stars.................................................. 06
2. Chapter 1: Melancholy I................................................................ 11
3. Chapter 2: The Woman in Red.......................................................... 26
4. Chapter 3: The Bookseller............................................................. 38
5. Chapter 4: The Bridge of Death........................................................ 51
6. Chapter 5: Michalská Brána........................................................... 59
7. Chapter 6: La Tarta de Queso.........................................................69
8. Chapter 7: The Hanged Man........................................................... 49
9. Chapter 8: The Moon.................................................................. 86
10. Chapter 9: The City of Seven Hills ................................................. 99
11. Chapter 10: Roots................................................................... 119
12. Epilogue: Finis Gloriae Mundi....................................................... 136

# Prologue
# Under the Heat of Dead Stars
*Press Clavis.*

I don't think I have any good memories of childhood. When this realization arose, during the psychoanalytic process, I remember a deep sadness filling me.

I was a curious child, always looking to understand the world around me. I have a peculiar memory of when, at the age of 6 or 7, I tried to unravel the mystery of time. I questioned how my father's wristwatch always showed a few minutes more than the one on the kitchen wall. "Is his watch in the future?" he thought. It was days before someone explained to me that the clocks could be "adjusted", but this only fueled my intrigue.

Another memory takes me to a science class, when I was 10 or 11 years old. Amid the deafening noise of a crowded room, the teacher said that the fire needs oxygen to exist. I asked, therefore: "So the Sun is surrounded by oxygen, since it burns?" His answer was vague; She only insisted that there is no oxygen in space. Perhaps astrophysics was too distant knowledge for the reality of a public school in the confines of the city of São Paulo. Months later, with the help of internet access, I understood on my own the process of nuclear fusion of the Sun.

I don't know where this curiosity came from. It seems to be something intrinsic, something that didn't come from my parents. They had no education, no curiosity. They lived on traumas, mistakes and addictions. And the addiction that most marked my life and that of my brothers was alcoholism.

My father, although an alcoholic, was almost a shadow. Silent and shy, he only found courage in drunkenness, and then he vented about his frustrations, the troubled relationship with my mother or the traumas of his own childhood. Until one day, in my adolescence, he succumbed to psychosis.

My mother, on the other hand, always knew how to express herself, whether she was sober or not. And she was good at it, especially at hurting with words. If I had to describe her, as a child, I would be like "an angry woman."

His anger seemed uncontrollable. I remember once, when I was about 5 years old, when I was punched while drinking water. The reason? She didn't like how my lips were in the glass.

But growing up in this environment was not entirely useless. A mother like mine would never raise weak children, and a father like mine would serve as a clear example of what I should never be.

I remember a time when I fought at school and my mother went to pick me up. To my surprise, she said: "Miguel, every time you fight at school, I'm going to hit you. If you lose the fight, I'll beat you twice more."

Where I emerged, in fact, there was no room for failure. I was nobody, and there was no possible way but to achieve something, because getting worse seemed impossible. Or, at least, that's what I thought; until I realized, in adolescence, that many where I came from, in the same conditions as me, found a much worse future.

But I felt that it wasn't for me. I wanted more. I just didn't know how much more. Perhaps this was my original sin.

---

As a teenager, I realized that I had a natural aptitude for mathematics. This set me apart from the others and, who knows, it could be my chance for the future.

With some effort, I got a scholarship to attend college at night, while working during the day to pay the rent, since my father, in one of his psychotic episodes, kicked me out of the house.

With more dedication, scholarships and some money saved, I did postgraduate studies and moved to another city, close to where my older brother and his children lived.

My life has stabilized. I had built a solid and relatively well-paid career. I had my nephews around, I practiced Aikido, I had a girlfriend who loved me, and whom I also loved. But despite this stability, something was missing. The curiosity that has always accompanied me was not limited to questions of Astrophysics or Time. Since I was a child, existential questions have haunted me, those that haunt humanity per se: "Where do we come from?", "Where are we going?", "Does God exist?".

These questions were never a priority in a difficult childhood, but they were always there, latent. And I have never accepted simplistic or religious answers without critical examination.

While studying business and statistics, I also devoted myself to the study of ancient religions and the occult. The scientific method had always been my basis, and I was determined to apply it to the occult sciences. I wanted answers that would justify my origin, my pain, the hidden nature of reality, and whatever existed before life and after death.

My search led me to join esoteric societies, some with political influence, others with centuries of Hermetic tradition. I conquered degrees within these orders, learned secrets and rituals, but, deep down, I still felt like Faust: an ignorant person, no closer to understanding the universe.

In this time of *excessive stability*, melancholy took hold of me. The death of a close friend of one of these orders devastated me, and my younger brother, who had recently lived with me, had moved to another city. The knowledge I accumulated seemed insufficient. Everything was still mythology, manifestations of archetypes. Old and dead gods, who were only reflections of the unconscious.

My relationship began to crumble under the weight of this emptiness. My work, once fraught with challenges, has become monotonous and boring. I expected that at any moment, Mephistopheles would appear offering *true knowledge* in exchange for my soul.

I realized that, deep down, I was still that slight boy, full of doubts and few certainties. I felt this internal heat, almost going out, but it was never enough to warm up. A fragile heat, like that of a dying star, agonizing at the end of its own existence.

I needed to do something about it. It was the strength of this sensation, that the star inside me, which illuminated my life and everything around me was dying, and that I urgently needed to act, to make some drastic decision, that began my Magnum Opus, the path to the Philosopher's Stone of the ancient alchemists, the journey of Jungian individuation, the secret Vitriol. For now, I was just a *stupid person* who wandered completely lost in the Pardes.

And I knew that this journey would bring some chaos. But, at least, it would be chaos with some order.

# Chapter 1
# Melancholy I
*II. Clavis.*

I needed direction, something that would tell me what to do. And, to the joy of psychoanalysts, and of Raul Seixas, this "guidance" came through a dream.

As a child, the same dream visited me several times. I walked through a verdant place, full of exotic flowers, until I came to a well with a spiral staircase that seemed to descend endlessly. It was always at this point that I woke up. It took me years to discover that this place was not just a figment of my imagination; it really existed, hidden among the hills of Sintra, Portugal.

Months before my brother's move, the dream returned, bringing with it a restlessness that did not leave me at peace. My mind could create countless theories to try to explain the repetition of that place in my unconscious, a place shrouded in ancient mysteries and symbols, linked to the Knights Templar and the Rosicrucians. Every detail of Quinta da Regaleira seemed to have been erected to echo these secrets.

But none of these theories gave me a rational or satisfactory answer. Even though I sympathize with the concepts of reincarnation, I have always been too skeptical to give myself completely to any religious belief.

The decision to abandon everything shouldn't have been easy, but it was. I don't know if it was just because of this dream, or something I still didn't understand.

Saying goodbye to the people I love was painful, of course. From the woman I loved, from my brothers, from my nephews. The shadow of doubt that I might never see them again weighed on me.

After organizing my finances, resigning and saying goodbye, I bought my ticket to Lisbon. I was ready to follow the path that my dreams indicated, even without knowing where it would end.

---

Lisbon is a city where the ancient and the modern dance in perfect sync, its hills covered in narrow cobblestone streets that wind like historical veins, connecting souls and stories through the centuries. At first glance, Lisbon is a mosaic of colors — blue and white tile facades glistening in the sun (possibly the most beautiful sunlight there is), wrought-iron balconies adorned with flowers, and the deep blue sky that seems to merge with the Tagus, the river that embraces it with enchantment and serenity.

As you walk through the streets, the sound of fado, melancholic and beautiful, escapes through the doors of the old taverns, impregnating the air with "saudade" — that untranslatable word that encapsulates the entire soul of Portuguese speakers.
At every corner, the city reveals a new surprise: a breathtaking view from a hidden viewpoint, where the houses

stretch like a carpet to the sparkling waters; a quiet square with a carved fountain, where time seems to slow down; or a Gothic cathedral, whose towers seem to touch the sky.

In the heart of Lisbon, stands the Castle of São Jorge, dominating the city from the top of its hill, its ancient walls guarding secrets of Moorish invasions and past glories. From there, the city's panorama unfolds, with the river meandering towards the Atlantic and the neighborhoods of Alfama and Mouraria stretching out at its feet, living labyrinths of alleys where colorful clothes sway in the wind on balconies.

The yellow cable cars, icons of the city, creak through the steep hills, connecting the neighborhoods like a living timeline. They cross places such as Baixa Pombalina, with its wide streets and geometric buildings rebuilt after the earthquake of 1755, to Chiado, where literary cafes and bookstores breathe the legacy of Fernando Pessoa and other poets who once roamed those streets.

At every step, Lisbon tells a story of audacious navigations, conquests and discoveries, reflected in the grandeur of the Belém Tower and the Jerónimos Monastery, whose stones seem to have been sculpted by the very waves that brought the adventurous spirit of the navigators back home.

But Lisbon does not live only in the past. Modernity pulsates in Parque das Nações, where contemporary buildings stand tall on the banks of the Tagus, and the city's vibrant culture is celebrated in every museum, art gallery and cultural event, where the traditional and the avant-garde meet. At night, the city glows with a soft light, its alleys and squares illuminated by old lanterns that cast mysterious shadows on the stone walls.

Lisbon is a place of encounters — between sea and land, between past and present, between dream and reality. It is an invitation to contemplation, to a deep dive into the memories that its streets hold, and at the same time, a breath of inspiration for those who are looking for something new, something magical, something that only a city like Lisbon can offer.

And it was in this very special environment that I found myself.
I stayed in Lisbon for a few days, strolling enchanted through its alleys and narrow streets, appreciating the difference in the light in this city, which in my personal theory was what made Lisbon so unique.
But the moment to follow my path was decided. Sintra is very close to Lisbon, and I should take the train and go there and literally find the place of my dreams.

And I found more than that.

Sintra is a city that seems to have emerged from the oldest and most mystical dreams, a haven of mist and magic nestled in the green hills of the mountains. Its winding and narrow streets rise and fall between lush palaces, enchanted castles and beautiful gardens, as if guided by an invisible hand that invites the visitor to get lost and, at the same time, to find something deep and secret.

As soon as you arrive, the air is different—cool and slightly humid, carrying the scent of centuries-old trees and the whisper of breezes passing through tall pine trees. Sintra is shrouded in a cloak of mystery, where nature and architecture intertwine in a harmonious dance, creating landscapes that seem to capture the essence of the sublime.

At the heart of this enchanted atmosphere, stands the National Palace of Sintra, with its white conical towers that dominate the landscape like sentinels of bygone eras. Its elegant and symmetrical façade guards halls adorned with tiles and painted ceilings, vestiges of a time when kings and queens strolled through its corridors.

But it is by climbing higher, on the slopes of the mountains, that the true fascination of Sintra is revealed. The Pena Palace, with its vibrant colors and almost surreal architecture, looks like a jewel carved into the hilltops, floating among clouds. Its towers and walls colored in shades of yellow, red and blue are a feast for the eyes, reflecting the romantic spirit that permeates the entire city. From the top of its balconies, the view extends to the Atlantic Ocean, vast and infinite, as if the earth itself were suspended between the sky and the sea.

Around Sintra, nature is wild and at the same time cultivated, as in the enchanted gardens of Quinta da Regaleira, where caves and fountains seem to hide mystical beings.

Every corner of the city is a reminder of a time when the spiritual and natural worlds walked side by side. The parks and woods, with their gnarled trees and mosses that sparkle in the soft light, are home to secret trails leading to forgotten places where silence reigns and the spirit can roam free.

The Moorish Castle, with its walls that wind through the ridges of the mountain, seems to echo stories of ancient battles and conquests. From its ruins, the city reveals itself below, a verdant tapestry dotted with palaces, churches, and villages. Sintra is a place of dreams, but also of history — a place where legends are woven into every stone, and where the present merges with the past in a fog full of sensations and mysticisms.

As the sun begins to set, the mist gently descends over the hills, and the city turns into an almost dreamlike realm, where time seems to be non-existent. The golden light of dusk bathes the buildings, and the long shadows that are cast through the streets look like mythical figures, guardians of ancient secrets.

Sintra is more than a city; It is a portal to another dimension, where nature, art, and the human spirit converge in a place that cannot simply be visited — it must be felt, explored in every detail, and above all, experienced as a return to the depths of a forgotten but ever-present dream.

Arriving at Quinta da Regaleira, which is in the heart of these green landscapes, I found myself dumbfounded. This neo-Manueline palace and its labyrinthine gardens seem to have been taken from a magical tale, where every stone and every plant whispers secrets from ancient times.

Upon entering the gates of the Quinta, you are immediately enveloped by a peculiar atmosphere. The palace, with its façade rich in details, features a fusion of Gothic, Renaissance and Manueline styles, with towers, battlements and gargoyles that seem to keep a close eye on visitors. The walls are adorned with arabesques carved into the stone, and the air is perfumed by the flowers of the surrounding gardens.

The gardens are a veritable labyrinth of surprises and esoteric symbolism. Winding paths lead the visitor through secret caves, bubbling fountains, and staircases that seem to descend to the very center of the Earth.

The soothing sound of rushing water accompanies the visitor at every step, from the hidden cascades to the serene lakes that reflect the blue sky. Ancient statues, hidden among centuries-old trees, silently look out at passers-by, while small bridges and stone walkways invite you to cross into hidden worlds beyond the lush greenery.

As the day progresses and the sunlight begins to soften, bathing everything in golden tones, Quinta da Regaleira seems to vibrate with a magical energy. Twilight brings a new air of uncertainty, as long shadows stretch across the paths and the palace becomes a romantic silhouette against the sky tinged with pink and orange.

Among the many surprises hidden in the gardens is the Chapel, with its delicate architecture and its details that seem to defy traditional notions of sacred space. Small but impressive, it reflects the mysticism that permeates the entire Quinta, with stained glass windows that project soft colors onto the stone floor, creating an atmosphere of stillness and contemplation. Around it, statues of mythical figures lurk among the vegetation, keepers of ancient secrets, silent witnesses of forgotten rituals.

In every corner, there is a story waiting to be discovered, a secret buried in the Masonic and alchemical symbols that adorn the property. Quinta da Regaleira is not just a place to be visited; It is a sanctuary of reflection, inner search and connection with the mysterious. She seems to invite each visitor to explore both the world around them and the depths of their own soul, making each visit a deeply personal and unforgettable experience.

The Initiation Well, located in the deep gardens of the Quinta, is more than an architectural structure — it is a symbolic portal to a spiritual and mystical journey. Seen from the outside, it could be mistaken for an ordinary well, but upon approaching its edge and looking down, the visitor is faced with a downward spiral that seems to be lost in the depths of the earth. The atmosphere there is charged with mystery, as if the very air vibrates with ancient stories.

The descent through the Initiatic Well is a transformative experience. The spiral staircase, carved out of stone and carefully weathered, takes the visitor to an underground world where sunlight becomes more and more distant. Each step, as part of an ancient ritual, seems to symbolize a stage of the inner journey—a journey into the unknown, into the depths of one's own soul and unconscious. The stone walls, covered with moss and moisture, give the feeling that time has really stopped there, that we are beyond the outside world, as if the well were a connection to past eras, when the occult and the spiritual dominated the human psyche.

Along the descent, small openings in the walls let light in, creating a play of shadows and reflections that increase the sense of the unknown. These glimpses of natural light, filtered through the vegetation that surrounds the well, illuminate the steps in an almost ethereal way, as if the light is guiding the way, while the growing darkness invites reflection.

The number of steps is not random. The structure is said to have been built with deep esoteric symbolism, representing Dante's nine circles of hell, or the levels of spiritual purification in ancient initiatory traditions. The journey through the well is both physical and metaphysical, inviting the visitor to reflect on the mysteries of life and death, rise and fall, light and dark.

At the bottom of the well, a compass rose is engraved on the stone floor, surrounded by a Templar cross, reinforcing the alchemical and spiritual symbolism that permeates the structure. There, in the heart of the earth, the visitor is confronted with absolute stillness, a deep silence that seems to echo within one's own mind. It is as if the well were a place of rebirth—a descent into darkness and then back into the light, wiser, more awake, more aware of the meanings surrounding existence.

The Initiatic Well does not have a single interpretation. Some see it as an allegory of death and spiritual rebirth, others as a path of initiation into the secrets of alchemy and initiatory orders. However, the experience is unique to each visitor. As you climb the spiral staircase again, each step towards the surface seems to carry with it a new perception, a new understanding of what it means to walk the path of self-knowledge.

When it finally emerges from darkness to light, the visitor is no longer the same. The Initiation Well, with its physical and symbolic depth, leaves an indelible mark on the soul, as if the earth itself had whispered its most ancient secrets, revealing fragments of a knowledge that surpasses time and space. It is a place of transformation—a space where the spiritual and the earthly meet, creating an unforgettable experience for both body and spirit.

I walked all over the place, felt all this mystical aura and vibrations. But it weighed on myself: "what am I looking for here?"

I walked through the beautiful caves, saw secret passages and was curious where they could take me and what could be hidden.

But I did not believe that in any of those caves there could be a chamber with the Holy Grail.

I left the Quinta and walked melancholy down the street of the main exit, towards the city center. I was wondering if all this movement was not just a need for a vacation and would become only a few sabbatical months, before returning to ordinary life, as stupid as before.

When I stopped in front of the Biester. I had read about this place in my research on Sintra. The place, which is immediately next to Quinta da Regaleira, with possible underground connections between one and the other, is even full of obscure stories, it even has an Initiation Chamber with tunnels that can connect to the Quinta and other chambers that may be long forgotten. It also has its gigantic garden, and the palace itself, is one of the most beautiful things in all of Europe.

The Biester Palace, which is hidden almost secretly on the way to the Quinta, manages to be just as surprising. It is a low-key gem, surrounded by ancient and surrounding forests. Its façade, marked by neo-Gothic elements, seems to emerge from the vegetation like a work of art sculpted by the nymphs themselves. With its detailed and elegant features, it carries an aura of mystery, showing that it holds deep secrets, whispered by the walls to the wind that blows gently between the centenary trees.

Built at the end of the nineteenth century, the Biester Palace was conceived as a haven of tranquility and contemplation, where the soul can get lost in its many architectural nuances. The building, with warm and ochre tones, features delicate towers and ornate windows, each with a special view of the lush gardens that surround it. As you approach, it is impossible not to notice the details carved in stone and iron, which recall ancient symbols, mixing the sacred and the profane, the historical and the esoteric.

The gardens surrounding the palace are like an enchanted labyrinth, where winding paths get lost among trees with dense leaves and rare flowers. Small lakes and discreet fountains emit the soothing sound of water, inviting meditation and solitude. There, among the vegetation, there are hidden caves and secret passages that evoke the same enigmatic spirit that hovers over all of Sintra, creating an invisible connection with the land and its mysticisms.

Inside, the Biester Palace definitely doesn't disappoint. Each room is a journey back in time, adorned with exquisite furniture and artistic details that reveal the influence of diverse cultural and aesthetic currents. Delicate chandeliers hang from the ceiling, spreading a soft light that dances on the carved wood-lined walls and fine tapestries. The expansive lounges, filled with windows, allow natural light to creep in delicately, blending the wild exterior with the refined elegance of the interior.

By climbing the spiral staircases, the visitor is led to an upper floor that offers majestic views of the hills of Sintra and, on clear days, the vast ocean in the distance.

This blend of interior and exterior, of cultivated beauty and untamed nature, defines the spirit of the Biester Palace — a place of contemplation and beauty, where time seems to fold in on itself, offering visitors an experience of deep serenity, shrouded in splendor.

The Biester Palace is an intimate corner, a hidden gem among the great wonders of Sintra. It represents the perfect fusion between the human and the natural, the esoteric and the romantic, being an irresistible invitation for those who wish to lose themselves in its atmosphere of stillness and enchantment, where every detail and every shadow tells a story.

But there are still more important details in the Palace. The Initiatory Chamber of the Biester Palace is a place of deep symbolism and mysticism, hidden inside this unique place. Upon entering its gates, the visitor is enveloped by an atmosphere of reverence. The chamber, a sacred and reserved space, was designed to evoke a sense of transcendence and connection with the invisible, a place where rituals of spiritual transformation and inner discovery were performed.
The light in the Initiatic Chamber is soft and indirect, streaming in through tall windows and colorful stained-glass windows that project mysterious patterns onto the carved walls.

The environment seems suspended, where every architectural detail suggests that this is not only a physical space, but also a place of deep meditation. The walls, adorned with esoteric symbols and mystical figures, seem to tell stories—stories that only those willing to open their minds can comprehend.

In the center of the chamber, a circular platform is surrounded by delicately carved stone pillars, symbolizing the union between the earthly and the spiritual. This center, as simple as it is powerful, is where the initiates placed themselves for rituals and meditations, as if the space itself invited deep silence and introspection. Each stone seems to carry the weight of centuries of occult knowledge, as if the voices of esoteric, mystics, and spiritual seekers echoed through its walls.

Above, the ceiling of the Initiatic Chamber is a work of art in itself, a symbolic sky represented by geometric shapes that refer to the stars, planets and mysteries of the cosmos. The feeling is that, by positioning himself in the center of the chamber, the initiate is in the heart of a larger universe, connected to the higher forces that guide spiritual evolution.

The light that descends from the ceiling seems to gently touch the person in the center, as if bathing the soul with a sacred and restorative energy.

The columns around the chamber are ornamented with motifs that refer to ancient orders, especially Rosicrucianism, reinforcing the idea that this is a space of revelation, of search for the deepest secrets of existence. On the floor, geometric patterns in black and white, like a chessboard, symbolize the eternal duality of life — good and evil, light and darkness, conscious and unconscious — essential elements in the initiatory journey.

The silence inside the chamber is palpable, almost tangible, as if the environment itself were protected by a veil of mystery. As you move within it, the sound of footsteps is muffled, creating the impression that space is more than just physical—it seems to flow between the visible and the invisible, between the present and the eternal. It is a place that invites silent contemplation, where the ordinary world loses its relevance and the focus turns entirely to interiority.

When I left the Initiatic Chamber, I realized how impossible it is to feel as before. The environment, so loaded with meaning, seems to have left an invisible mark on the soul, as if the experience within that sacred space had awakened something dormant.

The Initiatic Chamber of the Biester Palace is thus more than just a room—it is a portal to transformation, a place where the soul aligns with the cosmos, and the spirit soars in search of eternal truths.

Yes, I found amazing places in Sintra and about its Templar secrets. But *"what did I expect to find?"*.

I walked melancholy towards the train to Lisbon. After all, I was just on vacation.

# Chapter 2
# The Woman in Red
*III. Clavis.*

At night, Lisbon's Bairro Alto transforms into a world apart, vibrant and energetic, where the narrow cobblestone streets take on new life under the yellowish light of old lamps. The facades of the buildings, adorned with iron balconies and weathered tiles, seem more vivid under the darkness, revealing a discreet and decadent beauty, typical of Lisbon's charm.

The air is dense, loaded with the smell of food coming from taverns and restaurants, and with the mixture of perfumes and sounds of laughter and music that spills through the open doors of the bars.

The neighborhood, during the day, seems quiet and almost sleepy, but at nightfall, it awakens as if guided by an underground energy. Small groups of people gather on street corners, filling the streets with voices and stories that intertwine in the air, as if the city itself were celebrating. Fado, that melancholic and deep song, echoes in certain corners, escaping through the half-open doors of the fado houses that keep this tradition alive, with musicians and singers who express the soul of Lisbon through each note.

As the night progresses, Bairro Alto pulsates with its own rhythm. The cramped and intimate bars begin to overflow, and the streets become extensions of the establishments themselves. People drink wine, craft beers and cocktails, while spreading out on the sidewalks and stairs, occupying every available inch. The sound of lively conversations mixes with the electrifying rhythm of DJs playing in small clubs, where neon lights flicker and the environment becomes saturated with energy.

At the same time, there is something almost poetic about the ordered chaos that unfolds there. The contrast between the centuries-old streets, which have seen so many generations pass by, and the vibrant youth that now occupies every corner creates an atmosphere of fusion between the old and the new. It is as if Bairro Alto kept the essence of past times, but at the same time renewed itself every night, in a constant life cycle.

And even though the party is the protagonist, there are moments of stillness hidden in its alleys. As you step away from the busiest streets, you discover quiet corners, where the shadows of the trees sway softly under the light of the streetlights, and the distant sounds of the night become a murmur in the distance. There, in the midst of the hustle and bustle, it is possible to find serenity, as if the neighborhood wanted to offer a break to those looking for an unexpected moment of silence.

Bairro Alto is a kaleidoscope of experiences — from vibrant music to unexpected stillness, from smiles and chance encounters to a sense of belonging to something bigger. It is the beating heart of Lisbon's nightlife, where the city shows its most vivid face, and where time seems to dissolve into a continuous stream of joy, music and celebration.

I stopped at one of those bars that had the air of an authentic Irish pub. I ordered an Old Fashioned. After all, I needed to start enjoying my vacation.

When he was already finishing the drink, a tall and thin figure entered the door. She had long, brown hair, and everything about her made me think she was British. Next to her, a friend with dark curly hair and striking eyebrows.

Our gazes met for a moment, and I felt that rare spark, that discharge of attraction that comes only a few times in life.

A sudden heat ran through my body, my heart raced briefly, and a slight pulse of adrenaline made me look away. I turned to the bartender and ordered another drink, trying to seem oblivious to what had just happened.

They sat down at a nearby table, and with the music at a moderate volume, I heard fragments of what they were talking about. It seemed that they were celebrating something important, perhaps an interview that one of them had given to an American broadcaster, mentioning the success of a book she had published.

The woman in red got up, walked to the counter and stopped next to me to order two beers. As he waited, he turned towards me and, with a sly smile, said in impeccable English, but with a charming accent, which I could not identify:

"Do you always have this melancholy and mysterious air, or is tonight special?"

I felt my face heat up. I didn't expect her to start a conversation with me.

"Well... today is the night of the Full Moon, I think everything intensifies, doesn't it?" — I replied, trying to stay calm as I picked up my glass.

She smiled with a twinkle in her eye.

"First time in Lisbon, isn't it?"

I nodded.

"And what are you looking for? Everyone who ends up here is looking for something."

I was intrigued by the word "we were."

"The Holy Grail," I replied, in a tone of defiance.

She laughed out loud.

Her friend, at the table, watched us curiously.

"I thought the Grail had been lost in the mists of the European Middle Ages," she said, still with a smile, but there was something enigmatic about her tone.

It was at that moment that I realized: she was not European.

— "Write down my number. When you find him, call me," she said, handing me the phone so we could exchange contacts.

She returned to the table, and I finished my drink. I decided to go out and walk through the streets of Bairro Alto. As I walked, what she had said resonated in my mind: "lost in the Middle Ages." There was something in that sentence, something deeper, that echoed in my head like a riddle.

And Europe was full of ancient mysteries, disappeared alchemists, occult books, castles with their secret galleries. Maybe I should consider some of the myths I saw in these secret orders and keep looking for something, maybe not only in Portugal.

---

Days later, on one of my walks through Alfama, I passed in front of the Museum of the Roman Theater of Lisbon, and decided to enter.

I realized that there was an exhibition of paintings. Well, I rarely felt that sensation. Perhaps only when I saw the Trevi Fountain for the first time, or the Abduction of Proserpina, in the Borghese Gallery in Rome.

Barahona Possollo's paintings are a celebration that is both vibrant and deeply symbolic of the classical tradition of art, but with a contemporary sensibility and dark nuances. The Portuguese artist, known for his technical mastery, creates works that rescue the grandeur of the old masters

— in my view, he is the Portuguese Caravaggio — but with a modern and often enigmatic look.

His portraits and compositions are imbued with an almost mystical aura, where the dramatic use of light and shadow, along with obsessive attention to detail, capture the essence and soul of his subjects in a way that goes beyond mere physical representation.

Possollo uses an intensified realism, where every detail, from the texture of the skin to the complexity of the fabrics, is worked with an almost photographic precision, but which is not limited to the reproduction of reality. His figures, often placed in classical poses, seem to emerge from a timeless space, suspended between the present and a deeper, more symbolic dimension.

There is something introspective and ethereal in his portraits; The expressions of the characters portrayed seem to suggest untold stories, secrets kept behind penetrating and subtly emotionally charged gazes.

One of the most striking elements in his works is the dramatic use of chiaroscuro, a technique inherited from the Baroque masters, where the light focuses on the most significant elements of the composition, highlighting faces, hands, and symbolic objects, while the rest of the scene dissolves into deep and mysterious shadows.

This contrast accentuates the emotional intensity of the works, creating an atmosphere of mystery, almost Dantesque. The viewer is often led to contemplate not only the technical beauty of the painting, but also what it suggests beyond the visible, as if the figures were wrapped in a silent narrative, something that only they and the artist fully understand.

Possollo's themes often refer to classical and religious-mythical motifs, but always with a personal and unique interpretation. His depictions of saints, for example, are far from being mere icons of devotion. Instead, there is a certain air of vulnerability and reality that transforms these figures into complex human beings, full of internal conflicts.

He also explores the symbolic nature of objects—books, relics, crowns—that add layers of meaning to his compositions, suggesting hidden narratives and references to both Western and esoteric traditions.

Possollo seems to play with time in his art, merging eras and styles. His work, while evoking the Renaissance and the Baroque, has a contemporary quality that makes it relevant to the present. His paintings can be seen as a bridge between the great tradition of European painting and modern concerns and sensibilities, a dialogue between the past and the present that unfolds in each canvas.

Barahona Possollo's art is marked by an unsettling beauty, where technical virtuosity finds a psychological and symbolic depth. Each painting is a window into a world laden with hidden meanings, where light and shadow, history and myth, good and evil, the mundane and the spiritual, and even the erotic and the sacred intertwine in a fascinating play of meanings and emotions.

The effect those paintings had on me was heartbreaking. All that symbolism so beautifully was almost transcendental.
I remembered my studies of alchemy as teenagers, the medieval engravings full of hidden and forgotten symbols, which could indicate sacred knowledge.

If someone could express that in their art, anything was possible.
It was possible that alchemists had discovered Azoth, the Philosopher's Stone. It was possible that there were mysteries not yet understood by the vast majority of men.

And, enriching my eyes with those paintings, I remembered that I was not so far from the city where one of the most intriguing and enigmatic alchemists of all time possibly was, if he was still alive (over 200 years old).

Fulcanelli, one of the main figures of modern alchemy, if not the main one, surrounded by mysteries and myths that still inspire curiosity and speculation today. Known primarily for his alchemical writings, especially the works "The Mystery of the Cathedrals" and "The Philosophical Abodes," Fulcanelli is a figure shrouded in shadows—his true identity remains a carefully guarded secret, fueling theories and legends ranging from his possible immortality to involvement in secret societies.

The pseudonym by which the alchemist became known, has never been identified with certainty. Several theories have been proposed over the years, with some suggesting that he was a prominent French scientist or intellectual of the time, such as Jules Violle, Eugène Canseliet (his alleged disciple), or even the famous physicist Pierre Curie. Others believe that he could be an even older figure, who would have managed to prolong his own life through the elixir of immortality, something that many alchemists sought.

The absence of clear records about Fulcanelli and the almost supernatural nature of his figure gave rise to speculation that he had mastered the deepest secrets of alchemy — the transmutation of metals, the Philosopher's Stone and, above all, the power over death itself. His alleged ability to remain anonymous in a period of intense intellectual activity fueled rumors that he had achieved immortality.

Fulcanelli's two major works are complex and highly symbolic, focusing on the alchemical secrets hidden in Gothic structures and ancient architecture. He did not limit himself to theoretical discussions about the alchemical process, but connected the Great Arcanum with art and architecture, seeing in medieval cathedrals, such as Notre-Dame de Paris, true stone books, where the secrets of alchemy would be inscribed.

"The Mystery of the Cathedrals" explores the idea that the architects and builders of the great Gothic cathedrals were initiated into the mysteries of alchemy, and that the buildings themselves served as instruments of spiritual and esoteric teaching. Fulcanelli saw these cathedrals as physical representations of hermetic knowledge, where every detail—from sculptures to seemingly decorative symbols—concealed hidden meanings related to the alchemical process.

"The Philosophical Abodes" continues this line of thought, analyzing monuments, constructions and symbols that, according to him, incorporated alchemical knowledge. Fulcanelli suggested that these monuments served as guides for those able to interpret their secrets, leading them to the discovery of the Philosopher's Stone, which symbolizes spiritual and material transmutation.

The myth of Fulcanelli is not limited to his written work. He is said to have mysteriously disappeared after the publication of "The Philosophical Abodes", leaving his disciple Eugène Canseliet as the guardian of his secrets. Canseliet, in his writings, stated that Fulcanelli would have managed to carry out the great alchemical work, which, according to legend, would have given him power over death.

Another intriguing myth about Fulcanelli involves World War II. Nazi scientists are rumored to have sought Fulcanelli to obtain the secret of transmuting metals into gold or to use his knowledge in the creation of a weapon of mass destruction.

However, Fulcanelli would have disappeared, escaping all attempts at contact. Some reports even suggest that Fulcanelli would have warned his disciples about the dangers of nuclear energy before the detonation of the atomic bombs.

One of the most notable stories is Fulcanelli's alleged last appearance in Seville, where he supposedly resided. According to Canseliet, he would have met his master decades after his disappearance, in 1954, in Spain. On this occasion, Fulcanelli would have been noticeably younger than when he disappeared, fueling the legend that he had actually discovered the secret of immortality.

What makes Fulcanelli such an intriguing figure is not only the mystery of his identity, but the philosophical and symbolic depth of his work. Fulcanelli transcends purely materialistic alchemy—the transmutation of lead into gold—and explores spiritual alchemy, where the true transformation is that of the alchemist himself.

For Fulcanelli, cathedrals and monuments were not just architectural works, but profound symbols of the search for spiritual enlightenment and the understanding of the divine laws of the universe.

His legacy is shrouded in darkness, and he remains one of the most discussed and revered figures in the esoteric world, especially among those who see alchemy as not just a physical science, but a spiritual one.

Fulcanelli, whether he is a real person or a symbolic construction, represents the eternal search for hidden wisdom, for overcoming human limits and for the power to unravel the deepest mysteries of existence.

And apparently, I was still on that quest.

# Chapter 3
# The Bookseller
*IV. Clavis.*

I had left my hope of finding any "Holy Grail" or "Philosopher's Stone" in the depths of the Biester's Initiation Chamber. However, I made my way to Spain.

Seville is a city that pulsates with life, history and passion, where the past and the present intertwine around every corner. Located on the banks of the Guadalquivir River, the city seems eternally bathed in a golden light that highlights the beauty of its squares, churches and palaces.

Seville's skyline is dominated by the majestic Giralda, the tower that was once the minaret of a mosque and today stands as the symbol of a city marked by centuries of intertwined cultures. The cathedral, the largest Gothic church in the world, imposes its imposing presence in the heart of the city, with its stones that seem to tell stories of conquest, devotion and power.

The streets of Seville are a charming maze of narrow alleys and wide avenues, where everyday life takes place between the shade of orange trees and the sounds of lively conversations. The alleys of the Santa Cruz neighborhood, a former Jewish quarter, are a haven of tranquility, with their whitewashed houses, flowered balconies and hidden courtyards that invite you to take a quiet break. As you walk around, it's easy to get lost in the beauty of the details: the colorful tiles, the solid wood doors, the fountains that murmur softly in the midday heat.

The spirit of Seville is vibrant, passionate, and deeply rooted in its traditions. The city lives flamenco as if it were an extension of its soul. In every bar, in every tavern, you can feel the clapping of your hands and hear the melancholic touch of the guitar, accompanying voices that express the visceral and intense feeling of "cante jondo."

Seville breathes flamenco, and this distinctive art reflects the very character of the city: intense, passionate and, at the same time, deeply lyrical.

Seville's squares are the center of social life, especially the iconic Plaza de España, with its majestic semicircle that hugs a serene canal. There, during the day, families stroll, couples paddle through the calm waters, and visitors get lost in the richness of the tiles that represent the provinces of Spain. Next door, Parque de María Luisa offers a green and lush refuge, where fountains, sculptures and winding paths lead passers-by to moments of peace amidst the hustle and bustle of the city.

Seville is also a feast for the senses. Its taverns and tapas bars are places of meeting and celebration, where unique flavors of Andalusian cuisine are served in small portions that invite sharing. Iberian jamón, fresh gazpacho, fried fish — each dish is an expression of the land, local ingredients and tradition that passes down from generation to generation. At dusk, the outdoor tables fill with people enjoying a glass of wine or a refreshing beer, while the smell of food and the laughter of conversations fill the air.

Seville is, above all, a city of contrasts and harmony. The grandeur of its monuments, such as the Alcázar — a Moorish palace that looks like something out of the "Arabian Nights" with its marble courtyards, fragrant gardens and intricate mosaics — blends with the welcoming simplicity of the humblest streets. It is a city that honors its Arab, Jewish and Christian past, whose cultures have left deep marks, visible on every façade, in every church transformed into a mosque, in every traditional festival.

At the heart of it all is the Sevillian: warm, welcoming and proud of his land. Seville has a rhythm of its own, where time seems to slow down, especially during siesta afternoons, when the sun is relentless and the city plunges into lazy silence. But as night falls, the city awakens with vibrant energy, its streets filled with life, music, and celebration. Seville is a city that is lived intensely, with all the senses, a place where the past is present at every step, and where the future is celebrated with the same passion that has guided its soul for centuries.

Easter in Seville, more precisely Holy Week, is a celebration deeply rooted in the soul of the city, where faith and tradition intertwine in an atmosphere charged with intensity and reverence. During this week, Seville plunges into a dark and solemn setting, where religious mysticism expresses itself in a visual and emotional way, enveloping its inhabitants and visitors in an almost liturgical experience. It is a period in which the city, normally alive and vibrant, takes on a darker tone, and the processions take over the streets with an almost ceremonial weight, loaded with penance and devotion.

As night falls, Seville changes. The narrow and winding streets of the historic center, bathed in the flickering light of the lamps, become gloomy passages where shadows of hooded figures, the Nazarenes, stretch on the facades of the centenary buildings. Dressed in their long tunics and conical hoods that fully cover their faces, the Nazarenes walk in silent, unbroken rows, holding candles whose flickering flames seem to fight the darkness that envelops the city. The image of these penitents, hidden in their robes, creates an almost medieval atmosphere, evoking rituals of purification and sacrifice.

The silence that dominates the processions is oppressive. The sounds of everyday life seem to fade away, and the only thing you hear is the shuffling of Nazarenes' feet over the ancient stones and the funeral beating of drums, marking the slow, solemn rhythm. The trumpets echo through the narrow streets, their high-pitched sounds cutting through the heavy air, like a distant, almost macabre call, that seems to evoke something deeper and more primal. The streets are full of people, but the atmosphere is one of introspection and respect. Each face in the crowd reflects the weight of tradition unfolding before your eyes— a tradition that dates back centuries of history and devotion.

When the pasos — the huge floats that carry the images of Christ and the Virgin Mary — appear, the atmosphere changes. The figures of Christ, often sculpted with expressions of agony and suffering, viscerally recall martyrdom and death. The scenes of the Passion are depicted with an almost raw intensity, and the weight of the crucifixion is palpable in every detail of the floats, richly decorated with gold, slowly melting candles, and blood-red flowers. The Crucified Christ advances slowly through the streets, carried by the costaleros, whose bodies writhe under the crushing weight of the andor, invisible under the mantle of flowers and adornments.

The audience, crushed against the walls of the narrow streets, watches in an emotionally charged silence. Tears flow discreetly from the eyes of many, while the air is filled with murmurs of prayer and silent supplications.

The atmosphere is one of deep mourning and reflection—not only on Christ's suffering, but on one's own mortality and the sins that each one bears. The passage of the Crucified Christ seems to remind everyone of the inevitability of death, judgment and penance.

Right after Christ, comes the Sorrowful Virgin, the Mother of God wrapped in black and gold robes, with her face marked by the unbearable pain of the loss of her son.

The expression of despair on the Virgin's face, sculpted with astonishing realism, is an emotional blow to those watching. Every step she takes is followed by fixed gazes of devotion, and when a singer, hiding on one of the balconies of the narrow streets, the silence is broken by that piercing melody, a song of pain that reverberates through the dark alleys, intensifying the weight of the moment.

The candles that the Nazarenes carry project a dim light, partially illuminating their hidden faces, while the steps of the processions wind through alleys and squares, following the same path that for centuries was trodden by penitents and faithful. It is a march that crosses the heart of the city, but also seems to cross time, as if the souls of the dead and the living were there, mixed in the darkness, watching the unfolding of this ancestral ritual.

The darkest night of all is the dawn of Good Friday. The city remains in vigil, with the most important processions leaving during the deep night. The Christ of the Hermandad del Gran Poder and the Virgin Macarena are led through the streets in the midst of an almost sepulchral silence, broken only by the wails of the trumpets and the grave beating of the drums. It is as if time stopped, and Seville was transported to a threshold between life and death, between the sacred and the profane.

Holy Week in Seville isn't just a religious event — it's a dive into something primal and profound. It is a mixture of faith, mourning and hope, where the city covers itself with a cloak of darkness and contemplation, while the rituals of penance and devotion envelop the souls of all who witness the solemn grandeur of these processions.

I walked through that procession of ghostly but fascinating figures when my eyes were fixed on a replica of the Holy Shroud passing by. The buzz around me became a distant echo for a brief moment, while an unexpected curiosity enveloped me, mixed with a slight fear. Everything seemed to slow down, and for a few seconds, I disconnected from the crowd around me.

Then I was interrupted by the presence of a man much shorter than me. He was flawless in every way: snow-white hair, contrasting with his incredibly youthful, almost time-free skin. His shirt was immaculate white, and even his shoes sparkled as if they had never touched the ground. All this perfection caused me a strangeness, as if he did not belong to that chaotic scenario.

In a clear voice and without any accent that I could identify, he asked, in Spanish, as he pointed to the piece in front of me:

"Do you know what it is?"

Awakened from my reverie, I replied, in rusty Spanish:

"It is the Holy Shroud, the representation of the shroud that, they say, covered the body of Jesus."

He raised an eyebrow, as if this information was new to him.

"Ah... How interesting," he said, with a faint enigmatic smile, before turning and continuing on his way.

Before he turned, something caught my attention: hanging around his neck, a gold chain with a peculiar pendant—the mathematical symbol for "more." The sight baffled me. How could a Spaniard of that age, in a country historically so Catholic, not know the Holy Shroud? And what did that symbol mean? I was curious, but I continued on my way.

The next day, continuing my tour of Seville, until I was completely amazed where I had just arrived.

The Plaza de España is, without a doubt, one of the grandest and most enchanting settings in all of Spain, where history, art and architecture meet in a perfect harmony, perhaps without exaggeration. Inaugurated in 1929 for the Ibero-American Exposition, the square is a true masterpiece of regionalist architecture, mixing Renaissance and Moorish elements with traditional Spanish style, creating an apotheotic atmosphere that seems to evoke centuries of culture and tradition.

Upon entering the square, the first impression is of immensity. The vast semicircle, embraced by the monumental building that curves elegantly around the square, invites the visitor to immerse himself in a space of splendor and opulence. The symmetrical towers that flank the ends of the structure seem to watch over the site like sentinels, offering a majestic perspective of the Andalusian sky, which, at dusk, is tinged with gold, reflecting in the tranquil waters of the canals that wind through the square.

In the heart of Plaza de España, a large fountain emanates soothing sounds of running water, creating a mood of serenity that contrasts with the grandeur of the architecture. The movement of the water, reflecting the sunlight, adds an almost mystical dimension to the experience, as if each drop carries with it fragments of Seville's long and rich history. The visual effect is striking, especially when the sky lights up with the warm tones of dusk, making the square shine like a golden jewel.

The tiles that adorn the Plaza are undoubtedly one of its most fascinating features. Each province of Spain is represented by hand-painted tile panels that tell stories of their regions, creating a sense of unity and diversity at the same time. These colorful tiles not only embellish the space but also serve as a visual tribute to the country's rich artisanal tradition. Walking through the square and observing the details on each panel is like walking through a cultural map of Spain, with the vibrant architecture and colorful art serving as a bridge between the past and the present.

In addition to its architectural and artistic beauty, there is an almost mystical energy that hovers over the Plaza de España. The symmetry of the space, the curved lines of the building, and the gentle flow of the water create a perfect balance between nature and art, referring to the idea that this place is not just a physical construction, but a space for contemplation and spiritual harmony.

At night, the square is transformed. Soft lighting bathes the walls and towers, highlighting their imposing elegance against the starry sky. There is something almost mystical about the stillness that takes over the place when the flow of tourists subsides, and the Plaza de España transforms into a haven of beauty and serenity, where time seems to stand still, allowing the secrets and ancient stories of Seville to resonate in the stones and tiles.

Plaza de España is much more than just a square; it is a visual and architectural celebration of Spain's culture and history, a symbol of Seville and one of Andalusia's jewels. Every detail, from the colorful tiles to the imposing arches, is an invitation to lose yourself in its grandeur and immerse yourself in the narratives that it subtly tells in every corner, in every reflection, and in every step taken on its centuries-old stones.

I walked back to the central neighborhood of Seville and, between one small alley and another, I saw: an esoteric bookstore.

Well, I couldn't afford to miss the opportunity, could I!? I walked into the bookstore with a hesitant step, as if looking for more than just books on the old wooden shelves. The aroma of aged paper and leather permeated the air, bringing a strange sense of familiarity. Behind the counter, the bookseller—the same gray-haired, white-haired man I had met the day before, in front of the Shroud—was reading quietly, without looking up.

In a soft voice, but with a touch of precision, he broke the silence:

"Are you looking for something specific, or have you just let chance guide you here?" he said, this time in impeccable English.

I, intrigued by the enigmatic tone, responded with a slight challenge:

"Coincidences do not exist... just the illusion of coincidence."

He closed the book carefully, but continued to hold it, and then stared at me, his eyes curious as if probing something beyond words.

"Curious... Certain secrets often hide between the right pages. Sometimes in unlikely places," he paused, "We have a seeker here, haven't we?"

I had entered on impulse, but the strange feeling that this conversation was, at the very least, becoming quite curious.

— "I'm looking for answers... those that could explain life and the universe." — I confessed, in a tone that mixed poetry and irony.

The bookseller smiled, a discreet smile, almost as if sharing a secret.

"These answers... they are only found after crossing the bridge of death."

The "Bridge of Death"... I had already read about that curious place and its old engravings, which is in Lucerne. I interpreted, perhaps wrongly, that this was not a mere metaphor.

As I tried to process, my eyes landed on the book he was holding.

— "Basilius Valentinus... a remarkable alchemist, isn't it?"

For a brief moment, he seemed disconcerted by my sentence, but soon he composes himself.

"Yes, it's a biography that hasn't been published yet."

— "And is it interesting?"

"A lot. At this point in the narrative, he is about to cross St. Michael's Gate in Bratislava." — he said, quickly. Then, as if he wanted to change the subject, he added: "And what is your name, young man?"

"Miguel," I replied, sensing the irony in the air.

He smiled, a trace of sarcasm in his voice.

— "Coincidence? Or is it just another illusion?"

The bookseller shook his head, as if it were all just a coincidence, and pointed to the shelves full of old volumes.

"Make yourself comfortable, Michael."

I knew what I needed to do. First, cross the Bridge of Death. And then, if he managed to survive that, face the Gate of São Miguel.

# Chapter 4
# The Bridge of Death
*V. Clavis.*

Zurich, at first glance, is a city where modernity meets historic charm in perfect harmony. Situated on the shores of Lake Zurich, with the Alps in the background, the city combines contemporary efficiency with understated beauty, typical of Swiss cities. Known as the financial center of Switzerland and one of the cities with the best quality of life in the world, Zurich exudes a sense of order, prosperity and refined culture, but it also hides a historical and cultural depth that invites you to explore.

The Altstadt — the historic center of the city — is a charming network of narrow streets, lined with medieval and Renaissance buildings. Strolling through its cobblestone alleys is like traveling back in time, with every corner revealing a new colorful façade, an old carved watering hole or a cozy small square. Church towers tower over the skyline, especially the impressive Grossmünster tower duo, which dominates the Zurich panorama with its imposing Romanesque architecture and is linked to the origins of the Protestant Reformation in the city.

The city is famous for its museums, such as the Kunsthaus Zürich, home to one of the most important art collections in Europe, ranging from classical to contemporary masters. Zurich is also rich in green spaces, with manicured parks and the tranquil beauty of the lake, where locals and visitors alike stroll along the water's edge, enjoying the peaceful view and fresh air. In summer, the lakeshores become a lively getaway, with people swimming, sailing or simply relaxing in the sun.

In addition to the financial and historical side, Zurich is also a vibrant and innovative city with a dynamic cultural scene. Modern neighborhoods, such as Zürich-West, are filled with contemporary art, cool bars, and restaurants that blend Swiss tradition with global influences. This district, once an industrial area, has become a symbol of urban renewal, with warehouses converted into galleries, clubs and art spaces, while steel bridges and modern structures contrast with the city's more traditional architecture.

Zurich, with its gentle pace, balances the efficiency and richness of the modern world with a deep respect for history and nature. It is a city that reveals itself little by little, offering not only luxury and innovation, but also moments of contemplation and a silent beauty that conquers those who pass by.

But I was in a hurry to find Death. I took a brief tour of the main districts of Zurich, and went to the train station to take the train to Lucerne.

Lucerne is a city shrouded in lush beauty, situated on the shores of the serene Lake of the Four Cantons and surrounded by the mountains of the Swiss Alps, whose snow-capped peaks reflect in the calm waters. At first glance, Lucerne looks like a city straight out of a fairy tale, with its impressive natural scenery and historic buildings that seem to stand the test of time. The historic center preserves a medieval atmosphere, with cobbled streets and houses adorned with colorful facades and murals, which tell stories of an ancient and mystical Switzerland. But in addition to its pastoral beauty, Lucerne also has a dark side, especially visible in its iconic Chapel Bridge, the Bridge of Death, the Kapellbrücke.

The Kapellbrücke is the oldest covered wooden bridge in Europe, and crossing it is like walking down a corridor from the past. The bridge, which winds over the Reuss River with its sturdy wooden beams, offers an enchanting view of the rushing waters and mountains in the background, but what makes it truly unique are the enigmatic triangular engravings that adorn its interior. Painted during the seventeenth century, these images depict scenes from Lucerne's history, as well as religious themes and, markedly, rather somber depictions of Death.

As you walk under the cover of the bridge, the figures of Death appear in various forms, intertwined with scenes of everyday life and devotion. The presence of Death in these images is disturbing, but of a sinister beauty, reminding passers-by that she is a constant companion of life, always watching from a distance. The engravings show Death with his scythe, dancing with nobles, priests and peasants, a reminder of the inevitable end that awaits everyone, regardless of rank or wealth. These somber details, set in such a picturesque setting, create a fascinating contrast between Lucerne's external tranquility and awareness of the transience of life.

Each painted wooden panel seems to whisper an ancient warning, a reminder of the times of plague and war that once plagued Europe, and how death was a constant and visible presence in medieval life. The bridge, with its waters rushing below, offers a poignant metaphor: Like the river, life flows inevitably toward its end, and the course cannot be changed.

Even wrapped in beauty and tranquility, Lucerne has this darker vein, symbolized by the engravings on the bridge. This duality is what makes the city even more fascinating: the balance between the natural beauty of the Alps, the serene lake, and the inescapable presence of death, portrayed so vividly and unsettlingly. Lucerne, with its medieval towers and majestic mountains, is a city where past and present, the beautiful and the dark, coexist in perfect harmony.

I had lunch in one of the beautiful restaurants that were in front of the river and, from my view, such a majestic bridge.
As I ate, I wondered what I expected to find when I crossed the bridge.

After finishing my meal, accompanied by an excellent Swedish beer, I walked melancholy towards the train to Zurich.

---

Taking the opportunity to get to know the small and narrow streets of the historic center of Zurich better, I found a gallery that stood out for its internal modernity and the historicity of the external adornments of the building in which it was, and I decided to enter.

Alphonse Mucha's art is not only synonymous with elegance, fluidity and an exuberant celebration of natural beauty, she became one of the icons of the Art Nouveau movement in the late nineteenth and early twentieth centuries. Her works, with undulating lines, soft colors and detailed ornamentation, capture an ideal of femininity, also blending the divine and the earthly in compositions that seem to transcend time.

Mucha has created a unique style, marked by rich decorative elements and a visual lyricism that is mainly manifested in his posters, stained glass, illustrations and paintings. Her images—of idealized women draped in halos of light and ornaments—evoke a sense of mysticism and spirituality, while at the same time serving as symbols of a new industrial and artistic era.

One of the most recognizable features of his art is beyond simply female depiction, but these often with serene faces and ethereal expressions, surrounded by natural elements such as flowers, stars, leaves, and vines. These women, who are the beating heart of his works, seem like mythological figures or muses, personifying abstract concepts such as nature, music and the seasons. At the same time, they carry a subtle and pure sensuality, far from any vulgarity.

Mucha often positioned these female figures in graceful poses and wrapped their bodies in drapes reminiscent of ancient Greek robes, reinforcing the feeling of timelessness. These decorative details, such as wreaths and circular shapes that often surround their heads like halos, refer to an almost religious tradition, as if they were pagan saints, or goddesses of modernity. Every line and curve seems carefully thought out to express harmony and beauty, and it is this visual harmony that makes his works so instantly recognizable and mesmerizing.

Mucha's work is known for its undulating lines and organic shapes that flow smoothly through the compositions. These lines snake through the images as if they were part of nature itself, evoking the sensation of movement, even in the most static figures. This visual fluidity is central to the Art Nouveau style, and Mucha was one of its undisputed masters.

Nature also plays a crucial role in his art, but always stylized in a decorative and symbolic way. Vine leaves, lush flowers, stars, and circular shapes are integrated into his compositions in an almost abstract way, creating a perfect fusion between the human figure and the natural world. This integration suggests a holistic view of the universe, where humans and nature are intrinsically interconnected.

The colors in Mucha's works are muted, almost ethereal, with a palette that often includes pastels of blue, pink, gold, and green. With these colors, he managed to create a delicate and at the same time luxurious environment, with a glow that evoked gold and precious stones. The hues he used were often enveloping and provided his figures with a luminous, almost metaphysical appearance.

The ornamentation in his art is another of his most striking traits. Every part of his compositions, from the women's hair to the patterns in the background, is adorned with a meticulous level of detail, as if each curve and line had been thought of as a jewel in an intricate tapestry. This attention to detail creates a sense of opulence, but without exaggeration — there is a balance between ornamental and minimalist that gives lightness to his compositions.

Mucha is perhaps best known for his theater and advertising posters, especially those created for actress Sarah Bernhardt, which made him famous in the late nineteenth century. They were works of art unto themselves, turning advertising into a respectable art form. From there, he worked on a vast array of projects, from magazine covers to calendars and packaging, always with his own distinctive style.

In addition to his commercial work, Mucha devoted himself to more ambitious works, such as the Slavic Cycle, a monumental series of 20 paintings that narrate the history and myth of the Slavic people. These grandiose works are marked by an epic sense, mixing symbolism with a historical and spiritual narrative.

Despite his commercial success, Mucha seemed to believe that art should serve a higher purpose, connecting the human being to the spiritual and the universal. He saw his creations as something that should elevate the soul, away from the pure materiality of the modern world. In many ways, her works are a synthesis between the mystical and the ornamental, as if every flower, line, or woman's face contained a hidden secret about the cosmos and the individual's place within it.

Alphonse Mucha, through his art, has managed to capture the essence of an era of transition between the ancient and the modern, celebrating beauty and nature, but always with an almost spiritual lightness. His legacy is not only visually enchanting, but deeply symbolic, leaving an indelible mark on both the art world, popular culture, and me at that time.

Contact with art was having more effect on me than bridges of death and supposed ancient alchemists. But I had to continue on my way, maybe there was more art there.

# Chapter 5
# Michalská Brána
*VI. Clavis.*

Bratislava, the Slovak capital, is a city that seems to have a peculiar charm at every turn of its narrow and historic streets, with an atmosphere that is both erudite and deeply rooted in its medieval past. Situated on the banks of the Danube River, Bratislava appears to be a city that, at first glance, reveals itself in a modest way, but as you explore its shady alleys and ancient monuments, it unfolds in layers of history and mysticism. Bratislava Castle, perched atop a hill, dominates the skyline with its white towers that contrast with the gray sky, like a solemn guardian watching the city below.

The historic center is compact, almost like a maze of streets paved with ancient stones, flanked by Baroque and Gothic buildings that have witnessed centuries of invasions, coronations and revolutions. As you walk through its streets, there is a constant sense of the past, as if the stones beneath your feet still carry the weight of the Roman legions that passed by, the Hungarian kings who were crowned in their churches, and the ghosts of a Central Europe marked by empires that rose and fell.

St. Martin's Cathedral, where many kings of Hungary were crowned, stands imposingly, with its tall tower that seems to pierce the sky. For centuries, this cathedral has been the spiritual heart of the city, and as you enter its doors, the air seems to change — it becomes denser, quieter, as if you are stepping away from the modern world and into a dimension of faith and history. Stained-glass windows cast colorful lights that dance on the cold stone walls, and the smell of incense still lingers, evoking memories of ancient ceremonies and whispered secrets.

Bratislava is a city of contrasts. The modern and the ancient meet in a peculiar dance, where glass and steel skyscrapers appear next to Renaissance buildings, but always with the weight of the past dominating the environment. St. Michael's Gate, the city's only remaining medieval gate, is a symbolic entrance to another time, and as you walk through it, it's as if you're crossing a portal into an ancient Bratislava, where legends and stories blend with reality.

The Danube River, meandering lazily along the city, offers a constant and silent presence. Its dark waters reflect the lights of the city at night, creating an almost dreamlike scenery, where the shadows of historic and modern buildings merge into the current. Along its banks, there is a heavy silence, interrupted only by the distant sound of a boat cutting through the waters or the murmur of tree leaves, as if the river holds the untold stories of Bratislava.

At night, the city takes on an even more mysterious aura. The narrow streets are almost deserted, and the gloomy alleys, illuminated only by the soft light of the lanterns, take on an almost spectral quality. Bratislava Castle, which by day looks just like a tourist attraction, at night transforms into a ghostly figure, with its towers plunged into darkness, and the distant lights of the city cast shadows on the surrounding hills. It's easy to imagine that the ancient stones of the castle still carry echoes of the conspiracies and battles that took place there, as if the past had never really gone away.

Bratislava is also a city where folklore and mysticism are deeply rooted. Stories of supernatural creatures, of ancient kings and of sorcerers, are still whispered by the older inhabitants. Certain streets and squares are said to be haunted by restless spirits, and the historic buildings, with their narrow windows and decrepit facades, seem to harbor shadows that remain untouched for centuries. There is something dark and at the same time fascinating about the way the city embraces its history and myths.

The Blue Church, with its almost otherworldly architecture, stands out among the austere buildings with its soft color and curved lines, as if it had emerged from another world. But even it, with all its graceful appearance, seems to hold secrets from times gone by, reflecting the very spirit of Bratislava: a city that is both beautiful and mysterious, with a story that unfolds in layers, revealing new details with each closer look.

Bratislava does not reveal its secrets easily, but those who walk its streets with watchful eyes and open hearts will feel the weight of history, the depth of its culture, and the echoes of bygone eras that still resonate on its ancient stones.

The Gate of St. Michael and its Tower, Michalská Brána, is one of the most emblematic and ancient structures in the city, and carries a mystical aura that dates back to the Middle Ages. It is the only one of the original fortified gates that has survived time, guarding the secrets of a medieval Bratislava, full of legends and hidden mysteries.

With its Gothic tower towering over the city, it feels like a silent guardian of history, connecting the present to the deep and esoteric past.

Built in the 14th century, St. Michael's Tower was once an essential part of Bratislava's defensive fortifications, erected to protect the city from invasion and control access through the walls. Today, at fifty meters tall, the tower offers an impressive view over the rooftops of the Old Town and the Danube River, a sight that, for some, symbolizes not only physical mastery but also the spiritual connection between earth and sky.

Upon entering through the gate, there is a sense of transition: of leaving behind the modern world and immersing yourself in a medieval Bratislava. The shadowy passage under the arch of the gate is narrow and steeped in history. Whispers of old stories seem to float in the air, as if the ghosts of times gone by still walk around.

The top of the Tower is crowned by a sculpture of St. Michael, the archangel who, in Christian tradition, leads the heavenly armies against the forces of darkness. The presence of St. Michael, often depicted as the protector against evil and defender of light, gives the tower a symbolic aura of spiritual protection. It is said that St. Michael was chosen not only to guard the physical entrance to the city, but also to watch over spiritual energies, repelling evil influences that could enter Bratislava.

Inside the tower, there is now a small museum that displays the history of the city's ancient fortifications. However, there are those who believe that deeper secrets lurk within the walls of the structure. There are legends that the tower was once used by alchemists and occult scholars, who would have carried out mystical experiments on the upper levels of the building, seeking to understand the secrets of the transmutation of metals and spiritual ascension.

Another mystical aspect of the Tower is related to the kilometer zero marker, located directly under the arch. This point marks distances to various capitals around the world, but for the more esoteric, it is considered an energetic center, a point of convergence of energy lines that run through the earth. Some believe that the tower is strategically positioned over one of these "power lines," connecting Bratislava to a hidden network of spiritual and powerful sites throughout Europe.

During the night, especially on full moon or foggy nights, the tower of São Miguel gains an even more mystical and almost otherworldly atmosphere. The faint light emanating from the tower seems to be absorbed by the surrounding shadows, and the ancient streets that surround it are shrouded in a deep silence, as if awaiting some magical or spectral event. Locals whisper about ghosts of medieval knights who supposedly guard the gate, appearing from time to time to protect the city against unseen forces.

St. Michael's Tower, with its stories of defense, alchemy, and spiritual protection, is a point of fascination for those seeking Bratislava's occult mysticism. More than just a historic door, it is a symbol of the ancient city — a keeper of mysteries, secret energies and the legends that continue to entangle this fascinating city.

But nothing more than that. I had gotten there really with no expectations of finding a scroll hidden inside the Tower that had the means to produce the Philosopher's Stone.

Decide to walk through this small and charming center of Bratislava, until you notice a strange movement, and find a bar that is literally secret, in a secret entrance.

This bar seemed straight out of the pages of a mystery novel, with an engaging and seductive atmosphere. Hidden in one of the narrow streets of the historic center, behind an ordinary and almost imperceptible façade, this place is a true sanctuary of the forbidden and the enigmatic, where the experience of entering is as exciting as that of drinking one of the artistic and innovative cocktails that the place offers.

There are no flashy signs or large advertisements; Finding the bar was in itself part of the adventure. To access the bar, you need to go through a disguised door or, in some cases, follow subtle clues that can be discovered by those who know the ancient streets of Bratislava. This mystery around the place makes the expectation grow with each step, and when you enter the space, you are faced with an intimate environment, decorated with a vintage and luxurious air that refers to the time of the speakeasies of the Prohibition Era.

The interior is a real hidden gem: dark walls, low and soft lighting, and leather furniture that invites relaxation.

Candles discreetly illuminate the environment, creating shadows that seem to hide ancient secrets. There's something almost mystical in the air—as if the place is steeped in stories of stealthy encounters and secret conversations. The bartenders, dressed elegantly, are true modern alchemists, who create cocktails that look more like magic potions.

The menu was a universe apart. Here, you won't just find drinks; Each cocktail is carefully prepared with a unique combination of rare and exotic ingredients, often inspired by esoteric traditions and flavors.

There are mysterious herbal concoctions, aged liqueurs, and artisanal spirits, many of which carry enigmatic names and references to Slovak and European history or mythology. The presentation of the drinks is also a sensory experience: crystal glasses, enveloping smoke, hand-carved ice — every detail is designed to transport you to another dimension.

This was not just a bar, but a place for secret meetings and exchanges of complicit glances, where conversations close to the ear are conducted with the backdrop of soft music, which completes the aura of exclusivity. Many say that it is a perfect place for those who are looking not only for a different night out, but also for those who want to explore the most mysterious and secret side of Bratislava.

Whether for those who love the mysticism of the past or for those who just want to lose themselves in a magical evening with magical cocktails, this was an unforgettable experience, full of hidden charm and a sense of discovery, as if they had found a secret that few dared to unravel.

And as I sat there, experiencing this environment, trying my drink, and listening to the music, I felt the gentle weight of what it would be like *to truly exist*. Without the haste that once imprisoned me, or without the expectations of others, and my own, shaping every step. Now, time seems more malleable, almost as if I could touch it and shape it to my *own will*. Each moment is a little denser, with more meaning, as if each experience was destined to be savored, and not simply lived out of obligation.

The first sip of that drink, cold and aromatic, tastes like a revelation. It wasn't just a drink, but a quiet ritual of connecting with myself. The breeze from the window that carries the scent of the trees seems to me like an ancient whisper, as if the world is trying to tell secrets that I am only now ready to hear.

The things I enjoy, which were once stealth indulgences, are now celebrations of a life I finally make a point of living. Read a book late into the night, without worrying about the dawn. Walking aimlessly, enjoying the way the sunlight spreads through the streets, making them more beautiful in a way I didn't see before. It's curious how what was once mundane now carries an aura of mystery, but without needing to be explained. The beauty was always there, waiting for me to perceive it, but my soul was not awake.

I have always been surrounded by details that previously escaped me. The texture of the old wood floor and its creaking footsteps, the echo of the music playing in the bar, the whispered conversations of strangers who pass by me as if they were shadows. They are not just events, but fragments of something bigger, a mosaic that I am only now beginning to understand. Is living, then, that? Recognize that life is not the big event we expected, but rather a series of intricately intertwined moments, as small as they are essential.

There is a certain freedom in finally allowing yourself to appreciate. Knowing that the simple act of being present, of taking a deep breath and observing the world around you, is enough.

And that, I realized at that moment, is the true richness of life. It's not about achievements or unattainable goals, but about allowing yourself to immerse yourself in the little things that make your heart beat with curiosity and satisfaction.

For the first time, I felt that I was where I should be: life could be good.

# Chapter 6
# La Tarta de Queso
*VII. Clavis.*

My flight back to Lisbon had been canceled. Definitively. My alternatives were to go to Madrid on a one-day stopover there, or a two-day stopover in Bilbao.

Bilbao, in the heart of the Basque Country, is a city that constantly reinvents itself, where industrial past meets cultural innovation in a vibrant mix of tradition and modernity. Nestled in the valley of the Nervión River, surrounded by green mountains and close to the Atlantic, Bilbao exudes a unique energy, marked by the harmonious coexistence between futuristic architecture and historic neighborhoods full of charm.

The most iconic symbol of this transformation is the Guggenheim Museum, a magnificent structure of titanium, glass and stone, designed by Frank Gehry, that seems to flow like a living sculpture by the river.

Not only has this museum put Bilbao on the global map of contemporary art, but it is also a landmark of the city's urban recovery, which has gone from a decaying industrial hub to a culturally pulsating metropolis. The Guggenheim's curves and angles reflect the city's audacity to reinvent itself, with its metal surfaces shimmering in the sun and creating a fascinating play of light and shadow. In addition, the Basques have one of the most enchanting and mysterious languages in all of history. Knowing this culture and linguistic particularity alone would be worth the tours in the country.

However, the heart of Bilbao remains rooted in the Casco Viejo, the old quarter, with its seven narrow streets, known as "Las Siete Calles", dating back to the Middle Ages. This labyrinth of cobblestone alleys is lined with cozy cafes, pintxos bars, and traditional shops, where the Basque past still lives on in the colorful facades and Gothic churches like the Cathedral of Santiago. As you stroll through these streets, it's easy to get lost in time, admiring the centuries-old architecture and breathing in the authentic and welcoming spirit of the city.

During the Middle Ages, Bilbao, as well as other cities on the maritime trade route, attracted travelers from all over the Mediterranean, and with them came not only riches but also esoteric ideas and practices. The city, with its strategic location, became a meeting place for alchemists and occult scholars who sought to unlock the secrets of the transmutation of metals and the creation of the Philosopher's Stone.

There are records that nobles and merchants of Bilbao sponsored alchemists, who worked in laboratories hidden deep within the city's manor houses. Some of these houses, in the Casco Viejo (the historic center), have esoteric symbols discreetly incorporated into their facades, such as engravings of snakes, triangles and geometric shapes that refer to hermetic symbology. Many believe that these symbols were placed there by Freemasons or alchemists, and that there are hidden meanings in the very organization of the ancient streets, which follow geometric patterns connected to sacred geometry.

The bridges that cross the Nervión River are witnesses to the evolution of Bilbao, connecting not only the banks of the city, but also symbolizing the union between the old and the new. The Puente Zubizuri, a futuristic creation by Santiago Calatrava, with its curvilinear shape and glass structure, is one of the most impressive, contrasting with the historic bridges that recall the city's industrial past. Each of them seems to tell a story, marking the continuous flow of change and adaptation that defines Bilbao.

The city is also a foodie's paradise, with its pintxos bars dotted around every corner, serving small culinary masterpieces that turn simple ingredients into something extraordinary. The Mercado de La Ribera, one of the largest indoor fairs in Europe, is the perfect place to experience the authentic flavors of the region, with its vibrant stands filled with fresh seafood, Basque sausages, and local cheeses. Bilbao's cuisine, like the city, is a fusion of local traditions with modern and innovative twists.

Bilbao is also a city that moves to the rhythm of Basque culture. The Basque language and identity are always present, from bilingual signs to local festivities.
The Aste Nagusia, one of the most important festivals, transforms the city with music, dance, and traditional events that reveal the pride and passion of the Basque people. At the same time, Bilbao is cosmopolitan, open to the world, with a vibrant arts and cultural scene that attracts people from all corners.

Surrounded by hills and mountains, Bilbao also offers easy access to nature. It's not uncommon to see locals walking along the green trails that surround the city, or descending to the beaches of the Bay of Biscay to surf and relax to the sound of the Atlantic waves.

Bilbao is a city in constant movement, which respects its past, but looks to the future with boldness and creativity. A metropolis that has been able to reinvent itself without losing its soul, where every corner reveals a new encounter between tradition and modernity, between the urban and the natural. It is this duality — the pride of its roots and the incessant desire to project itself into the future — that makes Bilbao a truly fascinating place.

But, more fascinating than the mysteries and unique beauties of this city, or the indelible pleasures that the most varied and good wines of the region and the artisanal pintxos could bring, there was one thing that had truly made me fall in love.

While I was in one of these restaurants, I noticed that I always left, almost in the form of a production line, pieces of a pie that seemed quite peculiar to me.

Basque queso tarta, also known as burnt cheese tart, is one of the most iconic and enchanting desserts in the Basque Country, famous for its caramelized exterior and surprisingly creamy flavor. Simple at first glance, this tart hides a wealth of textures and flavors that reveal themselves with each bite, combining the rusticity of Basque cuisine with an almost magical sophistication.

When looking at the cheese pie, the first thing that catches your eye is its dark and burnt crust, a result of the high temperature of the oven, which creates a caramelized and golden layer, with a slightly bitter touch that contrasts perfectly with the sweetness and creaminess of the interior.

This almost accidentally imperfect appearance, with jagged edges and cracks that naturally emerge during baking, only adds to its visual appeal, evoking something rustic and authentic, as if it came straight out of a traditional Basque kitchen.

But it's on the inside that the magic really happens. When you cut the first slice, the cheese melts slowly, revealing a silky, almost liquid texture in the center. The pie seems to merge with the dish, and the first bite brings a deep, enveloping flavor: a rich blend of cream cheese, with a slight acidity and a hint of vanilla.

The contrast between the burnt exterior and the smooth filling creates a unique sensory experience, with the crunch of the outer layer giving way to the sweetness and lightness of the interior.

The secret behind this pie lies in the simple ingredients — cream cheese, eggs, sugar and cream — which together are transformed into something sublime through the intense heat of the oven. Traditionally baked without a dough base, tarta is a perfect example of how Basque cuisine values the purity of flavors and the simplicity of processes. The high temperature not only caramelizes the top, but also cooks the pie unevenly, creating the different textures that are the hallmark of this spice.

Served warm or cold, Basque cheese tart doesn't need complicated accompaniments. Its beauty lies in its simplicity. However, in some variations, it can be accompanied by red fruits or a light fruit syrup, which complement the delicate flavor of the cheese without overshadowing its essence.

The first bite reveals the perfect contrast: the sweet bitterness of the top layer and the creamy softness of the center. It is a dessert that seems shrouded in a cloak of culinary mystery, which impresses with the depth of its flavors, despite its unpretentious appearance.

For two days I gave myself over to all these pleasures and sins of Bilbao. I savored that magnificent cuisine and its special wines.

If there was any metaphysical quest ever in the course of my existence, I no longer remembered.

---

That was fine until I drank a little more than half a bottle of a very good pistachio liqueur.

The first sensation of intoxication is barely perceptible—a subtle warmth that spreads through the body, as if the blood is slightly warmed from the inside, sliding through the veins with an abnormal rhythm. The world around seems to vibrate in a strange way, as if the air becomes thicker, muffled, and each sound is enveloped in a distant echo layer. The fingers, once nimble, now weigh down, as if they had been coated in lead, while the skin begins to tingle with an involuntary shiver, a silent warning signal that the body sends, too late.

Thoughts, once clear, become dense, shrouded in a fog that thickens with each breath. The tongue moves heavy in the mouth, and the words tangle before they even reach the lips. There is a metallic taste, almost sweet and bitter at the same time, which begins to take over the mouth, spreading like poison. The eyelids feel heavier and heavier, and even the simple act of keeping your eyes open becomes a silent struggle against the approaching darkness.

Then, the heat turns into a feeling of suffocation, as if the surrounding air is slowly being stolen, drop by drop. Breathing, which was automatic, now feels like a conscious effort—a distant command that the body ignores. The chest is heavy, and the heart, once strong and rhythmic, begins to beat erratically, beating too fast, then slowing down, like a drum failing. A cold sweat runs down his forehead, his hands tremble, and there is a moment when the body seems to float between two worlds, oscillating between lucidity and the abyss of unconsciousness.

The surrounding colors begin to distort, fragmenting into tones that make no sense, as if the space is slowly disintegrating. The walls seem to curve inward, and the faces—if there are faces nearby—become distant blurs, shapes without definition. The sound around it begins to fade, becoming a dull, distant noise, until everything turns to silence. A deep silence that resonates in the emptiness of the mind.

Vertigo takes over. The ground seems to give way underfoot, but there is no fall—just a vacuum, a feeling of floating in a timeless space. The body, now insensitive, no longer responds to commands. The heart slows down once more, pulsing in an irregular rhythm, each beat echoing in the head like a slow drum. The vision begins to fade in circles, darkening at the edges, until only shadows remain, and finally not even that.

In the final moment before succumbing, there is a strange calm—as if the mind surrenders. Fear dissipates, and what remains is only darkness, a deep and absolute nothingness, where the body does not feel, and thought ceases. The last spark of consciousness is a whisper, extinguished, drowned in a veil of silence. The fall is slow but inexorable, until darkness becomes everything, and the world dissolves into oblivion with no return.

My last transcendental experience was the Tarta de Queso. "Was it worth it?" – I thought – "Probably yes" – I replied out loud.

I believe he was delirious, because, while he fainted, at all times, he remembered the engravings of death on the bridge in Lucerne. "Is it now that I cross the Bridge of Death!?"

---

Since I was a child, I knew that I had some kind of allergy to nuts and chestnuts.

The typical stomach discomfort after eating, brief difficulty breathing, feeling of nausea and nausea, made me stay away from these typical spices of the Christmas seasons from a young age.

But this had never happened with pistachios. Perhaps I had not yet eaten the amount necessary to cause any reaction, or drunk the right amount of some liquor made of it until I had to be hospitalized for self-poisoning.

I remember one of the first times in my life that I had the typical feeling of allergy. It was one of the nights before Christmas.

In the house there was a Christmas tree filled with those lights that shine and that delight any child.
I was fascinated. I looked carefully at the vibrant colors, and tried to see how from that small thread connected in a hole in the wall I could pass all those colors so vibrant and intense.

I wanted those colors for myself as well. So I pulled the connector out of the socket a little bit and put my finger there. It was also not pleasant at all.

I woke up in the early evening of the next day. A very nice nurse told me what happened, which hospital I was in, explained to me the amount of medicine I took and the deeply unpleasant procedure I had to go through.

He felt that he had really come back from the dead. In fact, I felt even more dead than alive, but I knew I was alive by the amount and intensity of bad sensations I felt in my body, in my head and maybe even in my spirit.

And all I wanted was to go home.

# Chapter 7
# The Hanged Man
*VIII. Clavis.*

Back in Lisbon, I still felt very bad, I had unspeakable pain in places on my body that I didn't even remember having. The constant feeling of nausea and the possibility of vomiting were more present with me than the figure of Death in the engravings of the Bridge with his Plague patients. If there was a purgatory, it was mine.

Even weeks after the event, I was still constantly nauseated, and that day, too much to stay at home; and even with some difficulty to walk having to sit all the time, I decided to go to Praça do Comércio and from there walk to Rossio.

The Church of São Domingos, also known as Rossio Church, exudes a dark and mysterious aura that distinguishes it from any other temple in the city. As you cross its doors, you immediately feel that this is not a place of immaculate beauty, but of deep scars, both physical and spiritual. The first impression is that the church, once majestic, was a silent witness to a cataclysm that forever marked its existence.

The marks of the 1959 fire still dominate the interior, creating a scenario of desolation frozen in time. The thick, dark, singed columns that support the vaulted ceiling look like charred bones of a living structure that has withstood the devastation. They are not smooth and perfect as in other Baroque churches — they are deformed, with cracks that snake their surfaces, as if the heat had tried to bend them. Their reddish and black hues evoke something primitive, as if they were forged in the depths of the earth, bringing to mind an image of fire and destruction.

In addition to its history of destruction by fire, the Church of St. Dominic has been the scene of other dark episodes in Lisbon's history, including the horrific massacres of Jews in 1506, where thousands were killed in the streets around the church. This historical charge is reflected in the heavy and contemplative atmosphere of the place, a space where faith and mourning coexist, creating an energy that seems to transcend the present.

The ceiling is low, heavy, like an oppressive presence that seems to descend on visitors, while the remains of the vaults are scarred by time and fire, with parts of the stone shattered and weakened by heat. There is a sense of heaviness in the air, almost as if the place is imbued with an invisible force that holds the gaze and keeps visitors in a state of silent awe. The silence here is different, it is not just the absence of sound, but a heavy stillness, as if every wall and column still echoed the muffled screams of the fire that consumed them.

The walls, once lined with vibrant Baroque decorations, now bear deep scars. The black tone of the burnt surfaces gives it an almost lugubrious aspect, where the sunlight that passes through the stained glass windows seems timid, filtering through like a spectre, creating distorted shadows that dance along the walls. This dim light intensifies the atmosphere of mystery, causing the details of the church to appear and disappear in the dim light, as if the past is still trying to emerge from the darkness.

The cold stone floor seems to be impregnated with hidden stories. Each footstep echoes through the central nave, reverberating through the walls like whispers of ancient times. The feeling of walking there is ghostly — a strange mixture of presence and absence. The visitor is constantly reminded of the tragedies that marked this place, whether by the destructive fire or by the bloody events of history, such as the massacres of Jews in 1506, whose echoes seem to still resonate in the worn stones.

On the altar, in the midst of the destruction, there is a striking contrast: gilded and gleaming statues, almost untouched, look solemnly out at the devastated space, offering a vision of hope or perhaps resignation. The gold shines with a light that seems out of place, as if it no longer belonged to that gloomy setting, but insisted on remaining as a last remnant of divine light in a place where shadows dominate.

The side chapels, small and discreet, look like niches of secret devotion. Some images of saints, grimy with time and smoke, look on with empty eyes, witnessing silent prayers that echo in the environment. Candles flicker with a dim light, almost insignificant in the face of the dark vastness around them. The smell of melting wax and the cold humidity of the space add to the atmosphere of melancholy and introspection.

Visitors are often gripped by a sense of subtle discomfort, as if the space demands a different respect — deeper, almost darker. Here, it is not divine glory that shines forth, but resistance in the face of destruction. The Church of St. Dominic is, in a way, a place of eternal penance, where the beauty of the past has been consumed and replaced by a raw reminder of mortality and the inexorable force of time.

This is not a space of easy redemption or immediate comfort. It is a place of reflection on the fragility of life, where faith and pain coexist, where the sacred and the profane intertwine in the dark shadows and stone scars that never seem to heal.

The tragedy known as the Lisbon Massacre of 1506, also called the Massacre of São Domingos, is one of the darkest events in Portugal's history. It took place over three days in April 1506 and was marked by the massacre of thousands of Jewish converts to Christianity — the so-called New Christians — in the vicinity and inside the Church of São Domingos itself, near Rossio, in Lisbon. The event was driven by religious fanaticism, intolerance, and the social and economic tensions of the time.

At the end of the fifteenth century, Portugal, like many other European countries, was experiencing a period of great religious intolerance. In 1497, King Manuel I promulgated a decree ordering the forced conversion of Jews to Christianity, prohibiting the practice of Judaism in the kingdom. Those who refused conversion had to flee or face death. Jews who converted to Christianity came to be called New Christians, but many kept their Jewish religious practices secret. Although they were officially Christians, these New Christians were often suspected of practicing Judaism in secret, and as a result, they were constantly the target of discrimination and persecution by the "old" Christian population.

In 1506, Lisbon was facing a major social and economic crisis, aggravated by a severe drought and a plague epidemic. There was a climate of despair and fear, and the belief in divine punishments intensified. Religious tensions and popular dissatisfaction with the presence of the New Christians, seen as "heretics" and guilty of many evils, were at their peak.

The massacre was triggered by a seemingly insignificant incident inside St. Dominic's Church. During a mass on April 19, 1506, a procession of the faithful gathered to pray for rain, asking for a miracle that would put an end to the drought. At one point, a ray of light entered the church and illuminated the crucifix, which many of those present interpreted as a divine sign. However, a New Christian who was in the church expressed doubts about the miracle, suggesting that the light was just a natural effect of the sun.

That comment inflamed the crowd. Outraged, those present began to beat the man, accusing him of blasphemy. The violence quickly escalated, with the support of two Dominican friars who incited the crowd to persecute all the New Christians in the city, blaming them for the misfortunes that afflicted Lisbon. They promised indulgences to anyone who helped kill the "heretics." From that moment on, violence spread through the streets of Lisbon, and the massacre took on brutal proportions.

For three days, an angry mob roamed the streets of Lisbon, attacking, torturing and killing New Christians. Many were dragged out of their homes, beaten to death, burned alive or lynched in the street. Rossio Square became one of the main sites of carnage, where piles of bodies were burned in bonfires, and the Church of São Domingos served as the scene of atrocities. Witnesses at the time reported scenes of extreme brutality, with men, women and children being killed without mercy.

It is estimated that about 2,000 to 4,000 people were murdered in these three days of violence. The blind fury of the crowd and the complicity of part of the clergy and the population aggravated the intensity of the barbarism. The homes of the New Christians were ransacked, their possessions were stolen, and many who tried to flee were hunted like animals.

Today, a simple memorial on the façade of the church commemorates the massacre of 1506. The memorial consists of a small plaque with the inscription: "In memory of the victims of intolerance and religious fanaticism. Lisbon, April 1506." The interior of the church, with its scars of fire and destruction, seems to express in a somber way the suffering of so many lives lost and the tragedy of a blind hatred that marked the history of the city.

And it was in this environment that I found myself. Sitting in that old and gloomy church, without hope, with my economic reserves crumbling and melancholy reigning in my being.

I no longer had veiled hints and hidden paths to follow, but I had realized one very important thing: I no longer had a place to return to.

# Chapter 8
# The Moon
*IX. Clavis.*

Many days later... I woke up in a dream. Consciousness was blurred, as if I were submerged in dark, thick waters, but at the same time, everything around me shone with a diffuse, oppressive light. A city with seven hills stretched out in front of me, immense, majestic, and strangely decadent. It was an ancient vision, a city that seemed to exist outside of time, but that, somehow, had always been with me. I felt an oppressive familiarity with those streets and buildings, as if I had walked through them in countless lives, without ever really getting anywhere.

The sky above was like a torn canvas, through which a cold light infiltrated, fragmented into deep shadows that did not correspond to physical forms. The sun? No, there was something different. An almost gray glow. He only revealed. The wind whistled like laments, as if the hills told forgotten stories, buried under the layers of the Earth, waiting for a voice to remember them.

Walked. Or I floated. The ground seemed distant, as if I moved effortlessly, disembodied. The winding streets wound around the hills, passing arches and ruins of civilizations I couldn't name. I saw statues of ancient gods, with empty eyes and faces worn by time. The symbology was undeniable, but everything escaped comprehension. He recognized some of the signs—fragments of hidden memories, perhaps of old sacred texts—but nothing was clear.

There were traces of a hidden truth, buried beneath the surface.

I passed through a vast square, with broken columns and twisted trees, and in the center, I saw a black lake, whose water seemed to absorb light instead of reflecting. I was drawn there, as if an invisible magnet led me to the center of that void.

As I approached, I noticed that there were figures at the water's edge. They were still, motionless, but their forms were vaguely recognizable—human, but not exactly human. They brought with them a sense of purpose that I couldn't unravel. Their faces were indistinct, but the eyes... Ah, the eyes were vast, as if they contained the cosmos itself, spinning slowly in infinite spirals.

One of them murmured. The voice had no clear origin, it echoed somewhere in my mind, like someone else's thought seeping into my own.

"A living one among the dead."

I tried to speak, but my mouth wouldn't move. The words were stuck in me, as if I wasn't allowed to break the gloomy silence of that place.

"There are two rivers," the figure continued, "only one of them has the echoes of what you already know but have forgotten."

I looked at the lake, trying to find some meaning in those dark waters. As I approached, I saw that its surface was no ordinary water. It reflected something deeper, an abyss where the hills seemed to distort and contort. There were visions in the reflection. I saw a battle, similar to the images of the Apocalypse—black horses riding in clouds of fire, crowds fleeing, and a tower in the distance, falling. But I also saw something calmer, a vast, endless plain, with golden fields and a river that stretched to the horizon.

"What is this?" I finally managed to ask, although without any voice. My mind projected the question, and the figures seemed to answer automatically, as if they were waiting.

"This is the end. It's the beginning."

The phrase reverberated inside me, like a hollow sound that couldn't dissipate. The Gita spoke of cycles, of samsara, the continuous birth and death, but there, the idea was palpable. I saw faces in the waters, my faces. I was a king, a beggar, a soldier. I saw the destruction of cities I did not recognize, and the peace of places I had never known.

One of the figures moved, slowly, as if defying time itself. The skeletal hand stood up and pointed to something in the distance. In the farthest hills, I saw a building. It looked like a cathedral, but at the same time, a fortress. Babylon? No, it was something more personal, something built from layers of my mind.

I walked, or I was taken. Time seemed to distort around me, the hills zooming in and out in a way that defied any notion of space. As I approached that building, I saw huge doors, open, but beyond them, there was only darkness.

The Apocalypse, as in the text, spoke of beasts and angels, of revelations that would destroy the world as we know it. But the darkness in front of me seemed less literal, more of a living metaphor. I was facing the unknown. The end of the illusion. Maybe, the end of me.

Entered.

Inside the cathedral, the space was immense, but without walls, without a ceiling. Only pillars that were lost in the darkness above. And there, in the center, I saw a figure sitting on a throne. A king? A god? His skin was golden, but his eyes were black as emptiness. He looked at me as if he had been waiting for millennia for that moment. I felt an enormous weight, as if I was facing something that transcends the human, something that I could destroy with a simple thought.

He spoke, but not with words. It was a knowledge that gushed directly into my mind, as if it were transmitting something ancient, a truth that I have always carried, but never understood.

"The city is falling."

"Which city?" I thought, but I already knew the answer. It was all the cities. It was my inner city, the hills that made up my own psyche, each representing a piece of my life, my choices and losses.

I felt a growing pressure, a tension that threatened to explode. It was as if my own being was about to be disintegrated, divided into tiny fragments.

He stood up and began to walk towards me, each step echoing through the void. When he was finally close enough, he held out his hand. And in it, I saw a flame. Small, but intense. A flame that seemed to contain the power of a thousand suns.

When I touched the flame, everything disappeared. The city, the hills, the figures. It was just me, suspended in the void, and the flame, which now burned. It didn't burn. It only illuminated what was previously dark.

---

A palace shone in the distance, surrounded by gardens that looked as if they had been cultivated by gods, where exotic flowers bloomed in vibrant hues, their petals gleaming with starlight.

But as I approached the palace, the tone of beauty became dark. The flowers withered at the touch of the mist, and the sound of music turned into a lament, as if the earth were weeping for the losses and betrayals that had occurred in its bosom.

As I entered the palace, I saw walls adorned with tapestries that told stories of forbidden loves, bloody battles, and intertwined destinies. In the center, a circular room displayed a vast astrological map, where constellations shone with an intensity I had never seen. The signs moved slowly, as if they narrated a story of crossed destinies, of past lives, and future lives.

As he examined the map, a shadow cast over it, causing the constellations to become distorted and grotesque. It was an entity that rose, a representation of the transcendental — not destruction, but transformation. The entity said something that I couldn't comprehend, or can't remember, but I felt its voice reverberating like distant thunder.

When I looked back the palace crumbled into a spiral of sand. Reality had turned again, and he was now in a desert, but no longer alone. A crowd was forming, travelers from various parts of the world, each in search of something, each carrying his own weight.

Walking among them, I saw faces of people I knew, others I didn't recognize, but who looked familiar. Each carried a flame, an inner light that illuminated the darkness around him. Some were tired, others hopeful, but they were all moving towards the same goal, as if an invisible thread united them.

When I reached a bridge, the feeling that I was about to cross was not just physical; It was a metaphysical crossing between the known and the unknown. Each step showed me a version of myself that I didn't know, fragments of what I had been and what I could be.

In the middle of the bridge, a shadow again formed in front of me. It was the embodiment of fear—a monster that grew in size and shape, molding itself from all the insecurities I had harbored. He rose in a storm of darkness, whispering doubts and uncertainties that echoed in my mind.

"I'm not just a lost traveler; I am part of the infinite."

The bridge began to glow brightly, illuminating the path ahead, and I saw the shapes that had lurked in the darkness begin to dissipate.

On the other side of the bridge, people walked through streets that seemed eternal, interacting in harmony with the surrounding nature. Flowers sprouted from the ground, and fruit trees offered shade and sustenance.

I walked the streets, feeling the connection with every being around me. A sense of peace and tranquility flowed like a river between us, where each life was a drop in a vast ocean.

---

I woke up, now in my room, with the sun filtering through the window. The compass was by my side, pulsating with new energy. What I had experienced was not just a dream; It was a transformation. I stood up, and as I looked out the window, I saw the world around me with new eyes— like a seeker, a traveler in the eternal cycle of life.

A hill rose before me, and as I drew nearer, I perceived that there was no more in the wilderness around the city; There was an open door that led me to a familiar place. It was Parque Eduardo VII, where the trees formed a green labyrinth, and the sounds of the city blended into a symphony of life. However, the atmosphere was impregnated with an unsettling silence, as if the park were on the verge of something majestic.

In the center of the park, a fountain gushed clear water, but as I approached, I noticed that the water reflected not only my face, but also the images of my memories.

Now I found myself on a second hill, which manifested itself as an ancient castle. Upon entering, I noticed that the walls were covered in tapestries that depicted battles and victories, but also tragedies. Each tapestry seemed to tell a story, and the lifeless figures there watched me with empty eyes, as if waiting for the coming of a hero who would never arrive.

In the center of the castle, I found a war room, where a council of warriors discussed plans, each of them representing a facet of the internal struggle we all face. Among them was a well-known figure, Krishna, who watched serenely.

Soon I was on the third hill, where the ruins of a temple stood majestic but ravaged by time. The air was heavy with the energy of ancient rituals, and the ground reverberated with echoes of forgotten mantras. In the midst of the chaos, a figure emerged from among the shadows: Kali, the goddess of transformation.

Kali stepped closer and held out her hand, making a gesture that seemed to conjure the essence of the universe. The temple began to glow, and the ruins turned into a vibrant place where life pulsated everywhere.

With the emergence of a fourth hill, I found myself in an obscure cave, the entrance shrouded in mist. It was an oppressive feeling, as if the darkness was alive, absorbing all the light. Upon entering, the cave opened into a huge underground room where mythical beings danced in the shadows, representing the forces of light and darkness.

In the center of the room, a colossal figure rose: like a being made of light, an archangel, with wings that shone brightly. He looked at me, his gaze deep and compassionate.

As he spoke words I couldn't hear, shadows began to dance around me, and I saw ghostly figures, animal figures I had never seen before, and even cities that looked like they were from another civilization. It was an endless cycle of situations and causality.

As he left the cave, the scene changed again, and he now stood before the fifth hill, which manifested itself as a grove. The light filtered between the leaves, creating a spectacle of dancing colors. The sounds of nature filled the air, and I could smell the rain that was to come. In the heart of the woods, I found an immense tree, whose roots intertwined like serpents.

As I approached, I saw that the tree had golden leaves that shone brightly, and between the roots, a shadow seemed trapped, trying to emerge.

As I left the woods, a new scene unfolded before me, and I was now on a snowy mountain. The air was fresh and pure, and as I looked down, I saw the immensity of the world below me. Every step I took was a challenge not to fall.

Upon reaching the top of the hill, the scene changed once more, and now I was back in Lisbon, at an elevated point where the seven hills were drawn in the soft light of the sunset. The memories of the hills still resonated in my mind and heart.

I looked around me and saw people walking, each of them carrying giant mirrors, which reflected completely distorted images of what they were supposed to reflect.

For some reason I decided to walk in the opposite direction of these people, until I reached a garden, whose leaves of the trees and plants had a deep dark green.

I continued walking and, with each step, the trees and leaves seemed to get closer and closer to me, in an attempt to imprison me, I began to have a brief feeling of despair.

When, continuing on my way, the trees and leaves looked as if they were going to crush me, I came out into an open field, with a giant, gleaming tree, the top of which seemed to extend above the clouds and continue through the universe.

I had a vision of the tree almost like a top, it seemed to be divided into ten parts, and the first and lowest part was a vibrant tapestry of life.

Every detail was exact and realistic, from the sound of birds going about their morning routine to the whisper of the wind caressing the leaves of the trees. I felt the texture of the ground beneath my feet, the warmth of the sun on my skin and the scent of wet earth, the aroma of new life. It was the embodiment of all that existed, and for a moment, I was lost in the wonder of the physical world.

On the surface, this was a realm of matter, but as I looked more closely, I realized that each element there was a reflection of the subtler energies that sustained it. Just as sunlight turns into heat, the energy of this tapestry was a manifestation of the upper parts of the tree, connecting each of its ends.

A fig blossom opened before me, and all around it, I could see the cycle of life and death in action. The ephemeral beauty of life was a constant reminder that every moment is precious, and that death is just a transformation. The flower was a symbol, a reminder that what manifests must also dissolve. Just as day becomes night, and life turns to death, each of us must learn to accept impermanence.

As I left the flower, the light began to intensify, and I was projected into another room. Here, the air was more ethereal, and the forms became fluid, almost as if I were inside a great river. The atmosphere was impregnated with images, symbols, and emotions, each an expression of the underlying reality.

It seemed that every thought I had, every emotion I felt, shaped the space around me. It was as if reality was constantly being created and recreated through my perceptions.

A series of mirrors appeared, similar to those walkers he had seen before, each reflecting different versions of a person, at different times and circumstances. I saw the curious child, the rebellious teenager, a melancholic adult. Each reflection brought up repressed emotions and forgotten memories.

After that, a colossal library materialized in front of me, with bookshelves that stretched to infinity. Ancient books and scrolls whispered secrets as I passed, secrets in languages I didn't understand, each book seemed to promise a revelation. When I opened one of them, I found an account of the ancient sages who discussed the meaning of life, love and death. His words resonated deeply with me, and I understood that wisdom is accumulated over time, being passed down from generation to generation.

As I walked, a green and gold light began to pulsate around me, replacing the library. A scene of war unfolded before me, with warriors facing reflections of themselves.

A vast field of roses opened before me, each more vibrant than the last. The red roses danced in the breeze, creating a symphony of red hues and scents. The room was transformed into a completely red room with an intense and powerful vibration, and the red pulsed like a heart in fury.

Then a lighted room appeared, as I entered the room the walls became darker, but no less beautiful and adorned; the shadows danced in a soft light, as if the darkness itself was telling stories.
A large bubbling cauldron was in the center, where ideas, visions, objects mingled and transformed.

As I looked intently into the cauldron, a vast field of stars and galaxies unfolded before me, and I realized that each star was a part of the shadow, which in that environment, formed a figure of my body.

"Every man and woman is a star," I recalled.

---

# Chapter 9
# The City of Seven Hills
*X. Clavis.*

When I awoke, I had the feeling that I had slept for two days. I hadn't even opened my eyes completely, I ran to my desk to get my notebook and start writing in as much detail as possible each part of this dream that gradually seemed more distant and gray.

The apocalyptic tones of my dream and the ambiguous sensations I had even hours after waking up reminded me of an ancient prophecy, still quite famous in some occult circles.

An enigmatic set of 112 mottos associated with each pope who would govern the Catholic Church, The Prophecy of St. Malachy is steeped in mystery and symbolism. With an origin dating back to the twelfth century, when the Irish saint Malachy had a vision while visiting Rome, this text has become a reference point for discussions about the future of the Church and the end times. Since its discovery in the late 16th century, prophecy has been the subject of varying interpretations, especially in relation to the last pope, a figure who, according to prophecies, will lead the Church in times of great tribulation.

The Prophecy would have been written in 1139, but its notoriety only grew from 1590, when it was published by cardinals who found it in an ancient manuscript. Cardinal Federico Borromeo was one of the first to draw attention to the text, which soon spread among the intellectuals of the time. Although the authenticity of the prophecy was questioned, its content resonated with the restlessness of a Church in crisis, especially in periods of wars and religious conflicts that marked the following centuries.

The phrases that make up the prophecy are cryptic descriptions of each pope, often with a subtle connection to their lives and papacies. Symbolic language and poetic traits make interpretations subjective, allowing diverse scholars and believers to make connections and traces of meaning, depending on the historical and cultural context in which they find themselves.

Each of the 112 mottos refers to a pope, and descriptions range from direct references to more vague symbolism. For instance:

Pope Pius IX: his motto "Crux de Cruce" (Cross of the Cross) refers to his strong defense of Catholic doctrine in times of secularization.

Pope Leo XIII: "De Laboribus Solis" (On the Work of the Sun) could be linked to his time of leadership during the Industrial Revolution and his encyclicals on social justice.

The mottos evoke images that may seem prophetic or ironic, leading to the creation of narratives that reflect the struggle of the Church in different eras. Each motto, while seemingly independent, fits into a larger puzzle, reflecting the continuity of Church history through difficulties.

The most intriguing figure in the Prophecy is the last pope, who is referred to as "Petrus Romanus." The motto associated with it is especially impactful:

"During the last persecution of the Holy Church, Petrus Romanus will shepherd his flock in the midst of many tribulations; after that, the City of Seven Hills will be destroyed, and the Terrible Judge will judge its people."

This motto resonates darkly, conjuring up images of apocalypse and destruction. The phrase "City of Seven Hills" refers directly to Rome, the heart of the Catholic Church and the center of Christendom for centuries. The prospect that the city could be destroyed raises questions about the permanence of the Church and the possibility of a spiritual collapse.

The figure of Petrus Romanus is full of symbolism. The name "Petrus", which means "stone" in Latin, refers to the apostle Peter, considered the first pope, and symbolizes the foundation of the Church. The addition of "Romanus" suggests a historical continuity, while at the same time implying a break with tradition.

What makes this prophecy even more fascinating is the timing of the prophecy. The "last persecution" is a concept that can be interpreted in many ways: as a period of growing hostility to the Christian faith, as religious persecutions throughout history, or even as a time of internal conflict within the Church. The combination of all these elements makes the figure of Petrus Romanus not only a leader, but a symbol of resistance in times of adversity.

Rome, with its seven hills—Aventine, Palatine, Capitoline, Quirinal, Viminal, Esquiline, and Celio—is not just a physical place, but a space laden with history and occult symbols. The city is a microcosm of human history, filled with ruins that speak of past glories and shadows that recall the falls of power. Each hill carries its own stories and myths, which reflect humanity's desire for transcendence, but also the inevitability of decadence.

During the Prophecy of St. Malachy, Rome was a place of great transformation, marked by battles of ideals and beliefs. Christians faced persecution under various emperors, and the narratives of martyrs and saints began to intertwine with the city's own history. This struggle for the survival of faith in the midst of a hostile environment echoes in Malachi's words and resonates to this day.

The mention of the "Terrible Judge" in the motto of Petrus Romanus intensifies the apocalyptic character of the prophecy. This figure can be associated with various traditions, from the final judgment described in the Book of Revelation to the conceptions of retribution and justice in different religions and mythologies. The Judge is not only a symbol of fear but also of hope for those who remain true to their faith, representing the possibility of redemption after the tribulation.

In moments of crisis, the figures of the Judge and salvation appear more frequently in religious discourses and collective narratives. The duality between fear and hope permeates reflections on the future of the Church and the destiny of humanity. Petrus Romanus, as the last pope, becomes an intermediary between Earth and Heaven, carrying on his shoulders the responsibility of guiding the faithful in dark times.

---

After so many symbolisms around me about the city of seven lines, I finally had to get to know this city that has always aroused my glimpse and curiosity.

The Eternal City, is a place where past and present dance in an intricate choreography, where the scars of history intertwine with everyday life. Upon crossing its boundaries, we are immediately transported to a universe where every stone and every monument murmurs secrets from a time when emperors ruled and gods were worshipped. The air carries the weight of the ages, a mixture of freedom and oppression, of light and shadow, that permeates its ancient streets.

I arrived on a calm morning, the sun bathed the cobblestone streets in a golden light, making the historic buildings shine as sentinels of time. The Roman Forum, with its majestic ruins, has shown itself to be a testament to the grandeur of the civilization that flourished there. The columns of the Temple of Saturn rise defiantly, while the echo of the footsteps of the ancient Romans still resonates in the weathered stones. Each corner reveals a new history, each shadow seems to carry the memory of an empire that spanned continents.

Walking through the narrow streets of Trastevere, I feel the pulse of modern life amidst the backdrop of the old. The cozy cafes and vibrant squares contrast with the majestic baroque churches, their facades adorned with sculptures that seem to come to life in the light of the setting sun. The voices of the locals mingle with the laughter of the tourists, creating a symphony of sounds that echoes through the air, while the aroma of fresh coffee and baked breads intertwine, creating an irresistible invitation for a break.

However, the beauty of Rome is interspersed with a certain melancholy. As you walk along Via della Conciliazione, the view of St. Peter's Basilica presents itself with its imposing dome, a masterpiece by Michelangelo. But behind its grandeur, there is an echo of conflicts and power struggles that have shaped the Church and the city. The Bernini columns that surround the square are a welcoming embrace, but also a reminder of the lives sacrificed in the name of faith and politics.

As the day progresses, the sky begins to tint with reddish hues, and the lights of the city begin to shine like stars in an earthly constellation. The Pantheon, with its majestic dome, invites reflection. Upon entering, the space is enveloping and solemn, with the light that penetrates through the oculus illuminating the sacred void. Here, the architecture becomes a metaphor for the search for the divine, and the reverence I feel is almost palpable. It is a place where the ancients and the moderns meet, where time seems to fade.

The Colosseum, imposing and worn, stands as a reminder of the bloody battles and spectacle of life and death. As I walk through its stands, I imagine the screams of the crowd, the adrenaline of the gladiators and the tension that permeated each combat. His story, filled with triumph and tragedy, resonates on the walls, making me wonder about the price of entertainment and the nature of humanity.

I saw a city that breathes, that lives and that dies, constantly reimagined and reinvented. As the night deepens, the noises of the day dissipate, giving way to a contemplative silence. The Tiber, winding through the city, reflects the lights of the buildings, while its waters murmur secrets that only the ancients would know. Walking along the riverside, I feel enveloped by a sense of solitude, as if each step were a journey through time.

And as the stars begin to twinkle in the night sky, I realize that Rome is more than a city; It is a symphony of stories, a tapestry of emotions and an ode to the human condition. It is a place where art and architecture become a reflection of the soul, where every corner reveals not only the beauty but also the complexity and duality of existence. Thus, Rome remains, eternally, as an enigma that fascinates and intrigues, an invitation to explore the depths of our own history and spirituality.

In Piazza Navona, beauty is shrouded in a cloak of nostalgia and mystery. The Fountain of the Four Rivers rises majestic, but on closer inspection, I realize that the waters seem to whisper ancient secrets. The carved figures, which represent the great rivers of the world, look at me with expressions that seem to capture the pain and glory of humanity. The Nile, with its cloth covering its head, hides its face in distrust, while the Danube, with a melancholy countenance, reflects on the currents of fate.

The alleys surrounding the square are narrow, almost claustrophobic, as if the city were trying to guard its mysteries. Cafes and restaurants, with their tables occupied by conversation and laughter, create a contrast between the joy and dark history that permeates the place. It is here that dreams intertwine with realities, and I cannot help but feel a strange presence, as if the souls of those who came before me still wander these stones.

The Piazza del Popolo, with its oval shape, is a portal to a darker world. The Flaminio Obelisk, which stands solemnly in the center, is a silent witness to times of achievement and pain. As I get closer, I feel a shiver run down my spine. The two twin churches, with their symmetrical facades, seem to look on with critical eyes, as if guarding the secrets of those who knelt in prayer under their roofs.

From the top of the Trinità dei Monti staircase, the view unfolds like a dark tale. The city's rooftops stretch out in a sea of reds and ochres, while sunlight drifts to make room for dim light. Here, the story is not just a succession of events, but a spiral of emotions—sadness, loss, hope—that intertwine like the roots of an ancient tree.

Finally I arrived at the place in Rome that I most wanted to know. Standing on the edge of the Tiber like a solemn watchman, Castel Sant'Angelo is a monument that encapsulates the duality of Rome's history—a fortress of power and a labyrinth of secrets. Initially built as the mausoleum of Emperor Hadrian, its robust, cylinder-shaped architecture seems to absorb sunlight, emitting an almost spectral aura as day turns to night.

When daylight fades and night settles in, the castle transforms into a place where past and present intertwine. The shadows lengthen and the stone walls, which have already witnessed intrigues, betrayals and redeemers, seem to vibrate with the voices of restless souls. An icy breeze whispers between the towers, bringing with it echoes of untold stories and secrets buried in the dark crypts that descend into the heart of the fortress.

At the top, the statue of Michael the Archangel, sword in hand, watches over the city like a divine sentinel. However, on closer look, his eyes seem to carry a weight of judgment. The heavy air that surrounds the castle is impregnated with a mixture of reverence and despair, as if the spirits of those who lived there were always lurking, ready to manifest themselves in moments of solitude.

The dark and narrow inner corridors are a labyrinth of cold stones that once resonated with the footsteps of popes, soldiers, and prisoners. The echo of the chains that dragged the condemned seems to still vibrate on the walls. Every door, every arch, is a reminder that this is not just a castle, but a place of transition—a space where life meets death, and where justice is often overshadowed by corruption.

The underground tunnels, which connect the castle to the Vatican, tell of an era of whispered secrets and treacherous alliances. The guards who served there were more than mere soldiers; they were guardians of an occult knowledge, part of a system that navigated the murky waters of power and betrayal. Rumor has it that some of these tunnels were never fully explored, remaining as pulsating veins of an enigmatic body that continues to exist beneath the city.

As the night wore on, the castle came alive with an almost palpable energy. The wind howls in the cracks of the walls, as if calling the spirits that dwell there. Visitors, armed with flashlights and curiosity, move like shadows, almost invisible under the moonlight reflecting off the damp stones. The stories told by guides, filled with ghosts and mysteries, echo in the minds of listeners, while the presence of the castle permeates the air.

People who venture into its walls speak of visions— flashes of a tumultuous past that plagues their consciences. The castle becomes a mirror of the anxieties and regrets of those who approach it. What was once a fortress of protection becomes a temple of reflection, where each visitor confronts their own shadows.

Castel Sant'Angelo, with its rich tapestry of history and myth, is a testament to the duality of the human condition. Its beauty is overshadowed by a cloak of melancholy, and the grandeur of its walls is almost suffocating, a constant reminder that power comes with a price.

As I walk away, shadows dance around, enveloping the castle in a dark embrace, as if protecting its secrets from a world that no longer understands its truths. The Tiber flows alongside, its waters reflecting the stars but also concealing stories that have never been told, while Castel Sant'Angelo continues to keep watch, an eternal guardian of Rome's mysteries.

The next morning began with a pale light filtering through the clouds, casting an ethereal glow over the domes and columns of St. Peter's Basilica. As soon as I crossed the immense doors, an air of awe enveloped me, as if the space itself was pulsating with the sacred history that inhabited its walls. The grandeur of the place was both dazzling and overwhelming; The cold stones, the polished marbles, every corner filled with symbolism and every fresco telling a story that transcended time. My footsteps echoed over the floor, resounding a whisper of uncertainty that I had brought back from my journey.

Catholic art, so glorified in its immensity, awakened in me a paradox of feelings. On the one hand, the history of the Church haunted me—the tortures, the inquisitions, the silencing of free thought. The blood of scientists and brilliant minds, shed in the name of a faith that feared knowledge. I remembered Galileo, Giordano Bruno, all the souls who were burned for questioning dogma, for seeking the truth in a world that preferred to live in ignorance. With a heavy heart, I reflected on the loss of many lives, the black mantle of oppression that had stretched for centuries.

But as I walked through the ornate hallways, the golden glow of Michelangelo's frescoes on the ceiling began to captivate me. The Creation of Adam, a sublime image that connects the divine and the human, became an invitation, a silent call to contemplation. I was an esotericist lost between the shadows of the past and the luminosity of art. What I saw, however, was not just the history of a religion, but the exaltation of the human spirit in search of beauty, truth, and love.

And so, as I went deeper into the Basilica, I realized that the war had been lost; The Catholics won. It was a bitter and strange victory, an achievement that had sealed a pact between the sublime and the profane. Art, now the true heritage of the sacred, flourished under the domination of the Church. Every sculpture, every painting, every musical note that reverberated in the vaults resonated with the greatness of the creative spirit, which, even under the aegis of an institution so often dark, managed to shine with an intensity that could not be erased.

The meticulously carved reliefs, the geometric perfection of the space, the nuances of light that danced on the marble walls—all of this spoke of a love for God and for man, an intrinsic connection that defied narratives of repression. It was a testament to what could emerge from the ashes of fear: beauty that shines through and uplifts, even in the midst of a never-ending struggle against darkness.

Suddenly, a soft melody was heard, echoing between the arches and the columns, transporting me to a state of slight sadness. It was sacred music, born from the voices of men and women who gave themselves to God through art. The chant resonated as a hymn to resilience, a reminder that, despite the horrors of the past, the light of human creativity was never completely extinguished. I was overcome by a feeling of gratitude for those who, even within an oppressive structure, managed to channel their spirituality into something transcendental.

That morning, as I stood under the majestic dome of St. Peter's, my fears began to dissipate. Catholic art was not only a reflection of religion, but a bridge that united past and future, a testimony of humanity's struggle and overcoming. Every brushstroke, every note, every stone was an act of resistance against oblivion, an ode to life in its fullness. The shadows that once threatened to extinguish the radiance of the human soul now served only to enhance its splendor.

In a sepulchral silence, almost feeling my lips sealed, I realized that my anger against the Church, while understandable, needed to be tempered with an appreciation for the most beautiful things that could emerge from its history. St. Peter's Basilica, in all its glory and pain, has become a symbol of the duality of existence. In its bosom, light and darkness coexisted, intertwined in a tangle of meanings that defied any attempt at simplification.

Thus, as I contemplated the details, the images of saints and martyrs adorning the walls, the beauty of the architecture unfolded before me like a revelation. I, a seeker in the midst of dreams and nightmares, found there an answer to my own journey. Ultimately, it was not about who had won or lost, but about how, in every trace of beauty, in every echo of art, there was the possibility of redemption.

The sun illuminated my path through one of the majestic stained glass windows, as if the heavens themselves were celebrating this new perspective. Each step, now, was a tribute to the art that resists, that speaks even in the midst of silence, an ode to all souls who, through pain, have found a way to express eternity.

They won the war, all that was left for any soul wronged during the Middle Ages was left to rest under the vault of art, sacred music and spectacular architecture full of fears and submission that religion still inflicted on some.

---

I crossed Rome on foot to the Borghese Gallery, which I found restful and splendid, hidden in the midst of the lush Borghese Gardens; where it emerged as a sanctuary of art that enchants and frightens. A Renaissance palace, with its white marble façade, stands as a fortress of beauty in a world often dominated by superficiality. As soon as you walk through the wrought-iron gates, you're transported to a realm where aesthetics and emotion intertwine, and each work seems to murmur secrets.

The architecture of the gallery, designed by Carlo Maderno in the early seventeenth century, is a splendor that reflects the grandeur of the era that conceived it. The rooms unfold like chapters in a book, each taking visitors to a new story. The ceilings are adorned with lush frescoes, which depict gods, heroes, and mythological figures, capturing a world where the divine and the human intertwine in complex ways. The light that enters through the large windows transforms the rooms into sanctuaries of contemplation, where beauty is almost palpable.

As you walk through the rooms, you are immediately enveloped by the presence of masterpieces by renowned artists. The Borghese Gallery houses one of the most important collections in Italy, with pieces by Caravaggio, Raphael, Bernini and many others. Each work, although rich in beauty, carries an emotional charge and a shadow of melancholy.

Walking among the works of great masters, I felt my heart beating, and a slight blurring in my vision. I had noticed, in the heart of the Gallery, between the opulence of marble and the delicacy of colors, the famous (for lack of better words to describe it) sculpture "The Abduction of Proserpina", created by the Baroque master Gian Lorenzo Bernini. This masterpiece is a testament to the power of art to capture not only the beauty but also the complexity of human emotions, while evoking a sense of darkness that runs through its mythological narrative.

The sculpture captures a dramatic and decisive moment in Roman mythology, where Hades, the god of the underworld, kidnaps Proserpina, the goddess of spring. The instant is frozen in an intense dynamic, where tension is perceptible. Proserpina, immortalized in marble, is depicted in a gesture of resistance and horror, while Hades, or Pluto to the Romans, strong and determined, lifts her in his arms, as if nature is about to be forced to give in to darkness.

Proserpina's eyes, wide in a mixture of surprise and terror, reflect a deep sadness. Her hands wriggle for support, as if to grasp something that is gone, while her flower – the symbol of spring – slips from her fingers. This flower, a symbol of life and hope, is left behind, suggesting the brutal transition from a luminous existence to the obscurity of the underworld.

Bernini, with his mastery of manipulating marble, captures not only the form but the essence of Proserpina's internal struggle. The light that falls on the sculpture highlights the contrast between being and non-being, the world of life and the realm of death. The dancing glow on the polished surfaces reveals the beauty, but also highlights the fragility of the human condition.

The folds of Proserpina's dress are meticulously carved, as if the fabric is about to fade into smoke. The way the tissue clings to your body is almost visceral, evoking a sense of vulnerability. The texture of the marble, at once soft and rigid, reflects the duality of its condition: the beauty of a goddess being tragically pulled into the darkness.

Pluto, in turn, is represented as a powerful, muscular figure, unperturbable in his desire. His eyes, though endowed with an intense expression, seem insensitive to Proserpina's suffering. The force of his presence is oppressive, a manifestation of the inevitable fate that awaits us all. It becomes a symbol not only of desire, but also of possession, of the consummation of life in a darkness that cannot be reversed.

The sculpture itself is a visual narrative, where shadows play a vital role. The shaded areas, created by the angles and the depth of the work, seem to pulsate with a life of their own. They form a cloak of mystery that surrounds the scene, as if the narrative itself were inserted in a larger plot of tragedies and inevitable destinies.

"The Abduction of Proserpina" is not just a story of love and loss; It is a reflection of the deepest human experiences – the struggle against fate, the search for freedom, and the inevitability of death. In Roman mythology, the abduction of Proserpina symbolizes the seasons: its descent into the underworld represents autumn and winter, while its return to the surface marks spring. This cycle, which repeats itself eternally, reminds us of the fragility of life and the inevitability of death.

The murmurs of the gallery around the sculpture, with visitors admiring the work, create a cacophony of voices that intertwine with the story of Proserpina, or Persephone.

Their expressions of awe and wonder resonate with the pain and beauty encapsulated in the stone. The gallery itself seems to breathe in unison, wrapped in a cloak of reverence for the past, a space where art is eternally alive, but also eternally trapped in a cycle of light and shadow.

The experience of observing The Abduction of Proserpina was an invitation to reflection. The sculpture is a mirror that reflects not only the story of a goddess, but also our own human condition. When faced with grief and loss, we are confronted with the inevitable question: how do we deal with the shadow that haunts us?

As the eyes lock on Proserpina's expression, there is a moment of identification.

The fragility, the pain and the beauty of their struggle become an echo of our own battles, of the inevitabilities that surround us.

Amidst the splendor of the Borghese Gallery, the shadow of history and emotion intertwine, creating a space of dark beauty that endures far beyond time.

Thus, the work remains not only as a work of art, but as a powerful symbol of the universal truths of life, a reminder that even in the most intense struggles, beauty can be found, even if shrouded in shadows.

As I left the Gallery, introspective about the effect that Bernini's art was having on me, I saw the winding paths are surrounded by classical statues and fountains that whisper the laments of antiquity in the gardens.

The tall trees formed a canopy that filters the sunlight, creating a play of light and shadow on the ground, evoking an almost dreamlike environment.

The tranquility of the garden quickly became unsettling.

The murmur of the water seems to murmur ancient secrets, and the shadows dancing on the leaves seemed like fleeting figures, as if the souls of the gallery's former inhabitants were always lurking, watching the passage of time.

At that moment I realized that I was in the lands of my ancestors and, perhaps influenced by Bernini's art, I decided to follow the route of my immigrant grandparents and great-grandparents from that country, to the city that I thought was their home.

I wanted to connect with this aspect of the depths of my soul and my ancestry.

# Chapter 10
# Roots
*XI. Clavis.*

I took the train heading north, and I was very sorry that I didn't pass through Florence.

Cremona, an ancient city on the banks of the Po River in the Lombardy region, is a place where time seems to follow its own rhythm, like the slow beat of a forgotten sonata. As you walk through its narrow, stone-paved streets, there is an almost palpable sense of history steeped in the facades of the buildings. The soft light of the late afternoon gives the Renaissance buildings an amber hue, while long, sinuous shadows stretch through the alleys, evoking an atmosphere of mystery and nostalgia.

In the center of the city, stands the imposing Torrazzo, a clock tower that dominates the skyline. At nearly 112 meters tall, it is one of the tallest medieval towers in Europe, and its presence is both a landmark and a silent watchman, watching the centuries go by. The bell echoes with a depth that seems to resonate in the souls of those who hear it, bringing to mind memories of times gone by, when the shadows of the power of the Church and medieval guilds still hung over the city.

Next to the Torrazzo, the Cathedral of Cremona is a jewel of Romanesque-Gothic architecture. Its walls, decorated with ancient frescoes, seem to carry the weight of centuries of prayers and mysteries. Entering its interior is like entering another world, where the light that filters through the colored stained glass windows transforms the environment into a mystical penumbra. There is a stillness there, a sense that time has been suspended. The eyes of the statues of saints seem to follow visitors, and the smell of incense and melting wax creates a heavy and contemplative atmosphere. It's the kind of place where secrets can lurk in the shadows and where the divine and the profane seem to meet in a silent dance.

Cremona, however, is not only famous for its architecture. The city carries a unique musical history, impregnated by the mystique of violin construction. In the sixteenth and seventeenth centuries, master luthiers such as Antonio Stradivari, Guarneri and Amati shaped the destiny of the city, creating instruments that echo to this day. Luthier workshops still exist in Cremona, and as you pass through the streets, you can hear the soft sound of strings being tuned, mixed with the rustle of the wind in the trees.

However, there is something almost unsettling about this legacy. Each violin built there carries a soul within it, say the most superstitious. Stradivari's instruments are rumored to have been made from fallen tree wood in forests surrounding deep, dark lakes on stormy nights. Some believe that playing one of these violins is to evoke the ghosts of composers and musicians who lived and died in the pursuit of sonic perfection. The Violin Museum, which houses the city's most precious instruments, has a reverent and almost religious air. Upon entering their rooms, the feeling of being surrounded by fragments of something larger than life is inescapable.

But Cremona is also a city of contrasts. Beneath the tranquility of modern life, there is a hidden melancholy, like an out-of-tune note in a perfect composition. As dusk falls over the city, street lights create a sense of isolation, as if the place itself holds deep secrets, unreachable to those who just pass by. In a city where harmony is venerated, the dissonance of past lives and occult events seems to lurk around every corner.

On the banks of the Po River, the scenery is equally full of somber beauty. The river, wide and serene, carries with it not only the water that has flowed for millennia, but also stories of disasters, floods and shipwrecks. It is said that, on certain nights, it is possible to hear the whispers of those who have drowned, as if the river holds the voices of the forgotten. The fog that rises from the Po at dawn or dusk gives the city a spectral aura, as if suspended between two worlds, that of the living and that of the dead.

And then there are the small details: the quiet squares where the wind whispers between the columns, the old cafes where the marble tables seem to have heard conversations from generations past, the streets that curve in unexpected ways, leading the visitor to get lost in their own thoughts. Cremona, despite its musical fame and rich history, is a city that keeps its secrets closely guarded, like an unfinished symphony, waiting to be revealed to anyone who has the patience and sensitivity to listen to its subtlest notes.

The region, especially the banks of the river, was the scene of an interesting battle of the Roman Empire, around 271 AD, which was one of the most decisive and violent events of the crisis of the third century of the Roman Empire, an era marked by barbarian invasions, internal usurpers and the fragmentation of the imperial borders. This confrontation, between Emperor Aurelian and the Alemanni, became a legendary battle—a clash between the disciplined order of Rome and the indomitable fury of the Germanic tribes. The setting was the fertile plain of the Po Valley, where the river flowed wide and winding, one of the most majestic waterways in Italy.

The dawn that preceded the combat was shrouded in a heavy, damp fog, hanging like a ghostly curtain over the field. The mist seemed to engulf everything around him, distorting sight and sound, as if the ground itself was preparing for the violence that would soon stain it with blood.

The Po River, with its calm, deep waters, meandered between the plains as a silent force and indifferent to the carnage that was about to occur. On its banks, the green of the fields seemed to vibrate with a treacherous calm, a terrible contrast to the fate that awaited the warriors on both sides.

The Roman legions, led by the ruthless Aurelian, were organized with military precision along the riverbank. Their armor shone in the gray morning light, and the sound of metal, mixed with the screams of the officers preparing their troops, reverberated like war music. The Roman shield wall, reinforced by spears, seemed insurmountable, a war machine designed to crush any opposition. The discipline, rigid training and tactical coolness of the Romans were their greatest weapons, forged in centuries of conquest and conflict.

On the horizon, a horde of barbarian warriors began to approach, and the sound of rude drums and tribal shouts announced their arrival. The Alemanni, with their stout bodies, animal skins, and jagged armor of leather and iron, represented savagery incarnate. They were formidable men, born and raised in hostile lands where survival depended on brutality and constant combat. His short swords and axes hung from ill-fitting belts, but his eyes shone with fierce confidence. Among them, rumors circulated that they had been guided there by omens, signs that the gods were on their side.

When the two armies first faced each other, the battlefield was filled with an unsettling silence, interrupted only by the wind blowing through the ranks. The distance between the forces was short, and the Po River was close enough that both sides could see its slow and steady current. It was as if the river itself was lurking, waiting to swallow those who fell in battle.

Then, like thunder that breaks the silence before the storm, Emperor Aurelian gave the order to advance. The Roman legions marched with inexorable precision, their shields crashing into each other, creating a wall of steel that seemed unbreakable. The Alemanni, by contrast, rushed forward with uncontrolled fury, rushing toward the Romans like a swarm of hungry wolves. The initial clash between the two forces was brutal—the sound of swords cutting flesh, the creaking of shields and armor being shattered, and the screams of wounded and dying men filled the air.

The battle quickly escalated into a massacre. The strength and momentum of the Alemanni were powerful, but their disorganization made them vulnerable to Roman thoroughness. The legionaries maintained their formation, pushing their shields forward and thrusting their spears with lethal precision, while the barbarians tried to break through the line with a mixture of desperation and rage. The ground soon became slippery with blood, and the metallic smell of death filled the battlefield, mixed with the odor of sweat and mud.

Aurelian, who was watching the carnage from a small elevation, was calm. He knew that the key to victory was patience, and when he realized that the Alemanni were beginning to hesitate, he ordered a devastating attack from his cavalry. The Roman knights, armed with curved swords and circular shields, descended upon the enemy flanks like a storm of steel and death. The cavalry made quick and efficient work, cutting down the Germanic warriors with ease and without mercy. The Alemanni, realizing that they were being surrounded, began to retreat disorderly toward the river.

The Po River, which until then had been a silent presence, became a major player in the unfolding of the tragedy. Desperate, the Germanic warriors tried to cross the river, hoping to escape the massacre. But the current, fueled by recent rains in the mountains, was strong and treacherous. Many of the barbarians, burdened by their armor and weapons, were swept away by the icy waters. Their hands raised for help soon disappeared from view, and their bodies sank into the depths, carried away by the relentless current.

The few who made it across the river alive met the same fate as their companions—the strategically placed Roman archers fired arrows toward the survivors, who fell lifeless on the opposite bank. The plain by the river was now covered with corpses, and the Dust flowed with a dark hue, as if it had absorbed the horror and blood of the battle.

When the battle was finally over, night began to fall over the battlefield, bringing with it an unsettling silence. The field, once green and fertile, was now littered with broken bodies, abandoned weapons, and the echo of the screams that had died down as the sun went down. The Po River, calm as before, seemed indifferent to the carnage it had witnessed. On its banks, crows began to arrive, attracted by the smell of death.

Aurelian had triumphed, and the Roman Empire, for the time being, was secure. However, the price of that victory would be marked in the waters of the Po forever. The river, silent and eternal, would continue its course, carrying with it the echoes of a brutal battle, where life and death danced side by side, under the indifferent gaze of the heavens.

Inspired by this atmosphere of battle and chaos, I decided to go to the commune of Cremona and find out more about my old name and the origins of my great-grandmother's family, who as far as we knew, came from that city.

In a quick computer search, the attendant informed me that the original birth records came from a nearby village, Pomenengo, a small commune located still in Lombardy.

Surrounded by vast fields of wheat and corn, its gentle hills stretch out under a sky often shrouded in low, gray clouds, as if the climate itself conspires to maintain the aura of mystery and isolation that surrounds the region.

The road that leads to Pomenengo winds through agricultural fields and ancient oak forests, almost like a natural corridor that prepares the traveler for the transition between the present and a past that, in many ways, still breathes in those lands. As you approach the city, the first sight that dominates the landscape is the bell tower of a medieval church, which rises above the faded terracotta roofs, like a lone sentinel.

The urban core of Pomenengo was modest, but full of details that reveal its deep roots in the history of Lombardy. Narrow streets, paved with jagged stones and worn by time, lead visitors through a maze of alleys where the silence is broken only by the occasional sound of church bells or the distant song of a bird. The houses, built in the traditional Lombard style, have stone and reddish brick facades, often covered with vines that seem to devour the walls with their verdant presence.

In the heart of the village, the church of St. Bartholomew is an imposing and somber presence. Erected in the thirteenth century, its rough stone walls and narrow Gothic windows create a sense of austerity.

The interior, dimly lit by a light filtering through the stained glass windows, is decorated with ancient frescoes, many of which are faded by time and humidity, giving the religious figures an almost spectral look. The air inside the church is dense and humid, carrying with it the smell of aged incense and cold stone, as if centuries of prayer and lamentation still hover in space.

On the margins of the village, the ruins of a medieval fortress resist, partially swallowed by the vegetation that surrounds them. The fortress is believed to have been built in the tenth century, during a period of conflicts and invasions that marked Lombardy. Its thick walls, now worn and partially collapsed, still hint at the solidity and strength that once protected its inhabitants from barbarian invaders and rivalries between feudal lords. The place is shrouded in an aura of mystery and abandonment, and many locals say that on winter nights, when the wind howls between the ancient stones, it is possible to hear the echoes of the battles that took place there, long ago.

The Pomenengo cemetery, located on the outskirts of the village, is another point that contributes to its gloomy atmosphere. There, between the moss-covered tombstones and rusty iron crosses, the silence is almost palpable, interrupted only by the rustling of leaves on the tall trees that surround the site. Some of the tombs are so old that the names engraved on the stones have been lost forever, transformed into illegible symbols that only death and oblivion understand.

There is an almost oppressive feeling of transience in that place, as if the land itself were aware of the weight of the centuries.

Pomenengo, despite his quietness and apparent simplicity, carries within himself the scars of a past full of uncertainties. The shadows of the old walls, the silence in the streets, and the constant murmur of the wind in the surrounding hills seem to tell stories of times when life was brutal and short, and where the line between the sacred and the profane was often blurred.

At nightfall, when the sky is tinged with a deep purple and the yellow lights of the street lamps dimly illuminate the ancient stones, the village took on an almost spectral quality. The shadows stretch across the walls of the houses and the deserted streets seem to whisper forgotten secrets, creating an unsettling sense that the past still lurks there, waiting to be discovered.

Pomenengo, with its melancholic beauty and its history marked by silence and oblivion, is a place where the present barely touches the surface of what once was. There is something dark but fascinating about its empty streets and old buildings—as if time itself had decided, in a pact with the earth and the wind, to keep that little piece of Italy stuck in an eternal twilight, where the past never dies, just waits in the shadows.

When I saw the castle that stood imposing over the city, a wave of emotions crossed me, the gentle breeze of Pomenengo enveloped me like a cloak, bringing with it the aroma of history and the fragrance of forgotten memories. The cobblestone streets, with their winding curves and the distant echo of laughter, seemed to tell stories of generations that, like shadows, intertwined with my own existence.

I felt an inexplicable connection, an invisible bond that united me to my great-grandparents, or to their parents and to the parents of their parents, whose footsteps had once walked those same streets. Tears welled up in my eyes, not out of sadness, but out of a deep sense of belonging. Each drop seemed to carry the weight of an ancestral history, a heritage that had transcended time. It was a silent acknowledgment, an affirmation that I wasn't just a visitor; I was part of that intricate tapestry that is life.

As the tears flowed, I realized that they were not just mine, but all the people in my lineage. They had lived, loved, and suffered, and each of them had left their mark on the world.

The castle, a silent witness to their journeys, seemed to vibrate with their voices, echoing memories of a past that, although distant, still pulsated in the veins of the city, and in my own. The whispers of the wind among the old trees seemed to bring back memories of children's laughter, family celebrations and moments of pain, but also of celebration.

The story of that tiny village lost in the middle of Italy was also mine. The struggle and resilience of my ancestors were inscribed on the stone walls, on the marks of time that told stories of survival, fear and love. I could almost see my great-grandmother, a brave immigrant to a distant and unknown country, young and dreamy, with her eyes full of hopes and longings, dreaming of the future I now represented. It was a gift and a burden at the same time, a reminder that life is made of choices and that, in each step I took, I also walked the path of each one who was in the past that I saw and that I did not see.

The castle, shrouded in shadows and light, seemed to carry a duality, reflecting both the beauty and sadness of existence.

The walls were witnesses of struggles and difficulties fought and of silent agreements, as well as the feelings that now inhabited my heart. There, standing before his majesty, I felt the vastness of the legacy that was left to me, as if each tear shed was an offering to the spirits that came before me.

That moment of transcendental connection not only evoked nostalgia, but also a deeper understanding of my own journey. It was an acknowledgment that while time moves forward and life takes us in unexpected directions, roots are never lost. They intertwine, forming an invisible network that binds us to a past that shapes who we are.

With teary eyes, I remained silent, listening to these voices of my ancestors. There was no need for words; the tears spoke for themselves. They were tears of gratitude, love and longing, a tribute to the legacy that, in some way, would always accompany me. Pomenengo was not just a city; It was a symbol of what is eternal in our lives: the memory, the heritage, the love and the struggle that endures through the generations.

The castle, like a timeless bloodline keeper, stood before me, and I, a timeline traveler, let melancholy merge with hope, knowing that the story I carried was ultimately a fragment of a greater whole, where every tear became part of life's dark and profound beauty.

---

I decided that I should spend at least one night on the town, and in the deep silence of that night, I was drawn into another dream that began as a whisper but quickly turned into a deafening grief. The darkness lifted, and, as if immersed in a veil of fog, I found myself in a house that seemed strange but at the same time familiar. The smell of old books and polished wood filled my nostrils, and the echo of distant voices reverberated on the walls.

I passed through a narrow corridor, where black and white photos adorned the walls. I approached a specific image: a woman with short, dark hair and piercing eyes, who watched me with an intensity that paralyzed me. Before I could process what that meant, a wave of memory came over me.

I was not the son of the woman who had raised me. In a stroke of revelation, I realized that I had been adopted.

The scene suddenly changed, and I found myself in a lighted room, where my parents, with tired and worried faces, argued in whispers. Sadness was stamped on their faces, but for me, there was something deeper, an almost palpable resentment. They were treating me as a burden, as a responsibility they wanted to discard. A lump formed in my throat as I realized that the little affection I had received could have been just an echo of the guilt they felt for not being my true parents. But this justified all the most of the bad actions and behaviors they both had with me in the past.

The memories of a childhood marked by schisms and pain began to intertwine with the devastating discovery. Every muffled scream, every look of reproach, and every harsh word I had heard from my parents now took shape and meaning. How could I have been so blind? My heart tightened as I remembered the nights when I hid under the covers, hoping that the silence would not be broken by an argument, by a scream that would remind me that I did not belong there.

I asked my parents who my mother was, and they replied, "Irina Petrovna." The image of her came to mind, and it was a strange and familiar image, like an echo of a past that I had never lived, but that still resonated within me. My desire to find her made me anguished, as if she were the answer to all the questions that haunted my soul. The dream began to fade, and the feeling of relief and sadness began to arise.

When I finally woke up, reality hit me like a storm. The day was clear, but the darkness of the dream still hung over me, like a shadow that does not dissipate with the light of the sun. The weight of the revelation overwhelmed me, and I couldn't help but let tears run down my face. The idea that I wasn't really the son of the woman who had raised me, to my unconscious, was the only way to explain the way she had treated me while I was a child. The dream, though only a glimpse of the truth, seemed more real than I would like to admit.

The echoes of last night reverberated in my mind: the coldness of my parents, the lack of affection, the emotional wounds that never healed. It was as if, by discovering the identity of "Irina Petrovna", this creation of my unconscious, I had also unearthed all my insecurities. The hope I had felt in imagining her was now just a painful reminder that I belonged nowhere. That it has not belonged anywhere for a long time.

As daylight invaded the room, I knew I needed to find a way to deal with this feeling. The pain of a childhood marked by rejection and the confusion of not knowing who I really was became a burden I couldn't carry any longer. I knew I needed to forgive not only my parents but also myself. To forgive, especially, the child who, without knowing it, sought love where there was none.

Irina Petrovna could be an unconscious symbol of pain and confusion, but she also represented an opportunity for rebirth. The dream had opened a door that I didn't remember existed, and as I crossed it, I realized that the journey of self-discovery began now.

With a deep sigh, I got up from the bed and stared at my reflection in the mirror. I was more than the shadows of the past. I needed to overcome the sadness and learn to forgive the memories that kept me imprisoned.

The dream could have been just an illusion, but the emotions it evoked were real. And with that, I would take the first step toward sovereignty and acceptance.

The expression on my face was not only one of sadness, but also of liberation. It was time to leave behind what didn't belong to me.

# Epilogue
# Finis Gloriae Mundi
*XII. Clavis.*

I felt the weight of years of searching finally converging. It was as if all the paths I had trodden—the travels through ancient cities, the possible esoteric encounters, and the hidden challenges—were closing in on a single point, a crossroads that transcended time and space. However, along with this, he felt the emptiness of the uncertainty of the future.

With every step I took through Sintra, Seville, Bratislava and so many other places, I realized that my walks were not just physical. I moved between worlds, a solitary pilgrim, hunting for truths that many had already given up looking for, others don't even start, others don't even need them. Now, back in Portugal, the air seemed dense, heavy with mysteries long forgotten, stored in every ruin, every stone. Mysteries that no longer mattered to me. It was as if the history of mankind itself was whispering, waiting to be revealed, and I no longer cared what it meant.

The wind was blowing softly from the hills of Sintra, but this time, I didn't feel the same comfort that had welcomed me before. Quinta da Regaleira, which had once been the portal to my deepest dreams and visions, now presented itself as a prison of dead questions. Time had turned that place into something almost unsettling. The Initiation Well, which I had descended with such eagerness before, called me back—a silent, profound plea that I could not ignore. He knew that the descent he had once made had not been complete. Something inside me still cried out for answers, for closure. This time, I knew that the steps would not only lead to the bottom of the earth, but to the bottom of myself.

As I walked through the worn stones of the garden, I felt that the Quinta was now alive, no longer a simple scenery. The shadows seemed longer, as if the place itself was aware of my presence and watching me. The surrounding vegetation was dense, and the air was laden with a sweet, almost intoxicating perfume, like the smell of old memories, of forgotten dreams.

As I approached the well, something inside me shuddered. The darkness below was as inviting as it was threatening, and with one last breath, I began my descent. Each step transported me back to the beginning of my journey, as if time was folded in on itself. The damp stones beneath my feet were cold but familiar, like the touch of something that had always been there, waiting to be rediscovered. Each rung of the tree of life, which had once been abstract esoteric concepts, was now tangible realities that I could almost touch, like a veil being slowly lifted.

Childhood memories mingled as I descended. I remembered the first time I felt the call of the occult, an uncontrollable curiosity, like a flame burning silently inside me. The voices of my masters, of the people I met, loved, and left, all echoed in my mind as the silent whisper resounded, no longer as a distant phrase, but as a command. "Visit the interior of the earth, and rectifying, you will find the hidden stone."

As I reached the bottom, I realized with painful clarity that the journey was never about others, it was never about the cities I visited or the masters I consulted. It's always been about me. To go down to the well was to go down to the bottom of my soul, and there, in that crushing silence, I began to understand that what I was looking for was never out. The hidden stone, the secret of alchemy, was my own transformation.

## 2. The City of Seven Hills

From Sintra, I was dragged in memories to Rome. There was something inevitable in Rome. The city had always called me back, even if I never really felt like I belonged to it. Rome was an enigma. With its ancient squares, its narrow streets and its imposing monuments, the city seemed alive, an entity that fed on stories and pasta. Rome has always been, for me, more than a city; It was a symbol, a key to the mysteries that I had always sought to unravel.

I walked through those squares, feeling the weight of the ages on my shoulders. It was as if every stone he stepped on carried centuries of hidden knowledge, tragedies and triumphs that shaped the history of humanity. I remember that as I approached St. Peter's Basilica, I felt a mixture of reverence and resentment. The towering dome cut through the sky like a finger pointing to the divine, but to me, it was more of a mark of earthly power. The Church, which for so long controlled the flow of knowledge, which hunted down scientists, burned witches, and persecuted those who dared to question its dogmas, was now the guardian of the most sublime art, of the richest history. "They won," I thought bitterly.

As I visualized myself again enjoying Michelangelo's Pietà, I felt a wave of emotions that almost knocked me down between the steps of the Well. The beauty of that work was almost unbearable, but mixed with it, there was the pain of knowing what was behind it all. The violence that preceded creation, the oppression that sustained the structure of that domain. The witch hunt, the torture of wise men, the secrets buried under the millennial stones of Rome. For many, the Vatican is the home of spirituality, but for me, it was the symbol of a lost knowledge, buried under millennia of control and power.

Looking at the sculpture, Mary holding the lifeless body of Christ, I realized that the Church itself, which claimed the monopoly of the spirit, also possessed the power over death.

"He who dominates death, dominates everything." Thought.

It was just one more proof that power over souls was always disputed, and in this game, occult knowledge was often sacrificed.

From Rome, I was drawn to Lucerne, where something darker awaited me. Crossing the Bridge of Death was more than a simple physical act, even more so what had happened in Bilbao. Every step I took under the engravings of Death with his scythe was a reminder that my own life was on the verge of a transmutation. The river below seemed to murmur ancient secrets, promises of something beyond material existence.

Each triangular panel of the bridge was a symbolic representation of life seeking its end, but to me, it signified the transitions I had experienced. Death, which had previously been only a distant concept, now approached me like an old friend, an inevitable transmutation. I had never feared death, but now it took on a new, more personal form. The crossing of the bridge in the two cities had been a rite of passage, a threshold that I really needed to cross.

As he continued, the darkness around him began to deepen.

The figures about the Well were no longer motionless; They moved in my peripheral vision, as if they were alive, dancing at the edge of my understanding. I felt that my being there was not a coincidence, but an inevitability.

And there I was, at the bottom of the steps, as at the beginning of everything, but I was definitely not so ignorant about the mysteries of the world, or my own.

And, looking up, I saw the top of the well being filled with the opaque light of the Sun of a beautiful gray day and, also, by that mystical mist that only Sintra can have; He knew he was a liberated man.

# About the Author

Born in 1992, Michael Sousa is Brazilian and has lived in Lisbon for a few years, holds a master's degree in International Trade from the European Business School in Barcelona, MBA in Strategic Management from FEA-RP USP, a degree in Computer Science and a specialist in Strategic Foresight. He has an extension in Applied Statistics and in Cost Management. He works with Project Management, Data Analysis and Market Intelligence. However, surrendering to his interest in Freudian theories, he also went to study Psychoanalysis at the Brazilian Institute of Clinical Psychoanalysis, and specialized in the subject and in clinical practice. When he doesn't spend his free time trying to develop his lousy artistic side, he finds himself studying the political-economic collapse of nations, psychoanalytic texts, or over many a quaint and curious volume of forgotten lore.

www.ingramcontent.com/pod-product-compliance
Lightning Source LLC
LaVergne TN
LVHW011950070526
838202LV00054B/4873